MW01487315

Also by Kyle Stone:

The Initiation of P.B.500
Rituals
Fantasy Board
Fire and Ice
The Hidden Slave
MENagerie

The
CITADEL

Kyle Stone

The Back Room

TORONTO, CANADA

The Back Room
is an imprint of Baskerville Books.

The Citadel
© 1994 Kyle Stone
© 2001 Kyle Stone

First published 1994 by Masquerade Books, New York

National Library of Canada Cataloguing in Publication Data

Stone, Kyle
    The citadel

ISBN: 0-9686776-4-9

    1. Title.

PS8587.T6628C5 2001   C813'.6   C2001-902024-4
PR9199.3.S8216C5 2001

Cover photo by Norman Hatton

Cover design work by Kevin Davies

Published by:
Baskerville Books
Box 19, 3561 Sheppard Avenue East
Toronto, Ontario, Canada M1T 3K8

www.baskervillebooks.com

Kyle Stone can be reached at www.kyle-stone.com

ONE

he vibration of the great air ship trembled through Micah like desire. The chamber they were in was large and unadorned. There was little besides the large round table that was bolted to the floor, as was the curving metal bench around it, and the immense banner covered with Kudite symbols that he couldn't yet interpret. In spite of their Spartan surroundings, there was an air of languor among the men. The feasting had been going on for hours, as they celebrated the successful outcome of their mission to Earth Base Gamma 1. Micah had played an important role in that success, but he doubted that many besides the leaders knew about it. To most, he was merely an alien love-slave branded by his master Attlad.

Still, he felt that his actions had earned him a special place in his master's esteem. His very presence, naked, his forehead painted with Kudite ceremonial paint, had provoked a real stir among the Terrans, and Attlad had gained valued status as a result with his own people. Everyone knew Micah could have escaped, yet here he was, kneeling at Attlad's feet, his face raised, mouth open for the wine that his master poured into him. The sweet heavy red liquid splashed over his chin and trickled down his smooth muscled chest, coating the gold nipple rings, the chain connecting them and the gold disk bearing his name, suspended from it. His throat worked, swallowing as fast as he could as he concentrated on following the unspoken orders to obey.

Attlad's dark face was smiling as he tipped the heavy wine sack forward, knowing his slave could take only so much, amused to see the blond Terran's face redden with the effort, the bronzed naked skin slick with the spilled wine, like the face of a greedy child.

"Chento," Attlad said, laughing.

Micah shuddered. The alien slave name still startled him at times, the soft intimate sound so different from the meaning, that was only a number. P.B. 500, personal bodyslave number 500 to a Kudite leader. All so impersonal. Regimented. Reducing him to a cipher. Hearing the name was meant to remind him that he was nothing but a possession, a prized possession at the moment, but nothing more.

Attlad withdrew the wine. As he leaned forward to talk to one of the leaders, he casually thrust his knee between the spread legs of his naked slave. Micah winced as his cock was pressed roughly against his master's laced boot. All the wine he had consumed was making him horny. He had been well trained in the months he had spent with the Kudites never to touch his own genitals or even his ass. Every part of him belonged to Attlad. Without his master, there was no release. Ever.

Micah pressed his shaved crotch against Attlad's leg, trying to sense if he had permission to bring himself off. His cock was hard and aching, had been for some time now as he watched the men laugh and talk from his position half under the table, watched hungrily as they casually displayed themselves, scratching their genitals. Some even stroked themselves to orgasm. It was a sight he was used to by now, especially after a period of great tension like the war games or a skirmish with another tribe. But he, too, needed release. Later he knew he would be used by Attlad, perhaps given by him to others for their pleasure. He was surprised it hadn't happened before now. But perhaps things were different because they were on the ship, going to the Citadel, the fabled city stronghold he had only heard vague rumours about. Even after all these months, it was difficult to understand the strange liquid language that flowed between the dark alien men. It lapped against his ears like water, but if he concentrated very hard, sometimes he could get the gist of what was being said. He knew the sign language that had been taught to him, as if he were nothing but an animal trained to obey hand signals, but none of the men bothered to sign unless they wanted something from a slave. Did the sign language come about because so many of the slaves spoke different languages?

Abruptly Attlad jerked his leg, throwing Micah off balance so that he sprawled on the metal floor. When he looked up, his master had pushed up his leather tunic and spread his legs. Impatiently he tugged at his slave's long fair hair, annoyed at having to remind Micah what was expected of him. It was Attlad's pleasure that was important, not his. He would find no release for a long time.

Micah scrambled to his knees and hastily undid the laced fastenings of his master's soft leather trousers. The warmth of the man's body beat against his skin. His nose drank in the mingled scents of spilled wine and leather and sweat, and that singular sharp sweetness that was Attlad's alone. Micah paused for just a moment, almost dizzy with desire. Then he buried his face in his master's hot crotch.

Attlad's dark wine red cock stirred as his slave's mouth opened against the sleeping shaft. Above his bent head, the men drank and laughed and joked together, knowing their leader's slave knelt between his legs, sucking greedily at his master's staff. The image of himself and Attlad, of the other men at the round metal table, floated in his mind, erotic in its evocative power. It was just one more of the images he would cherish, run over in him mind when he was alone, pining for contact, when in desperation he rubbed his own aching cock against the wall, the floor, trying to get relief and yet not break the rule. He knew this was like stealing from his master, but sometimes he couldn't bear it. Now he closed his eyes and ran his tongue along the salty shaft, pulling his long hair out of the way as he tilted his head to get closer, opening his mouth wide, his own saliva dripping over his chin as he laved the hardening cock. His tongue traced the small veins on the underside of the shaft, tasting the sour tang of urine.

Drawing back slightly, he straightened, balancing on his knees as the moist tip of Attlad's cock slid into his willing mouth. He paused, enjoying the moment until Attlad grabbed his hair and yanked his head closer, impaling his mouth on the hard flesh. He felt his face turn bright red as the great cock rammed the back of his throat, shutting off the air supply. His eyes opened wide in panic, rolling back imploringly. For an instant he thought he would pass out, then Attlad pulled back, just enough to let him breath, before filling his throat with his hot juices.

Micah drank greedily. When Attlad pulled out, he felt momentarily bereft without the great hot cock filling him. Attlad grabbed the wineskin and thrust it into his slave's mouth and tilted it back, back. Desperately Micah swallowed, his eyes shut in concentration. He heard the men laughing, felt the slick red wine bubbling over his chin, mingling with the sweat and the semen as it dribbled onto his chest.

When Attlad finally stopped, Micah was dizzy, drunk with sex and wine, exhausted from hours crouching at his master's feet. The noise was louder now, the men's tongue loosened with wine. Attlad casually laced up his trousers and pulled Micah out from under the table. With the hand signals Micah had learned to read so well, he told him to stand and wait.

"I have been bragging about you," he said, his hands moving smoothly in the air. "They say you aren't skilled enough to win against Dalet's slave. I say my Terran slave, my very own Nebula Warrior from Earth, will win any contest."

Micah blinked, trying to gather his wits about him. If they wanted him to fight, why had Attlad filled him with wine? He raised his hand to sign back.

"I am not used to fighting naked, Master. And I do not have my sword."

The others laughed, and he felt his face turn red. He was a warrior, every bit as skilled as they. He had been an officer in his former life. It was hard to remember that that made no difference, now. Except to Attlad. Someday they would fight side by side, Attlad had promised, as they lay entwined on the fine furs in his tent. Someday....

"You will fight naked this time, Chento. You will wrestle Dalet's slave. Now."

"But, master—"

His hand was knocked down, so he could no longer sign, and a small flagon of spiced oil was dashed over his shoulders. His senses reeled from the scents, usually associated with languid lovemaking, and it was difficult to pull his mind away from soft thoughts to fighting. He knew how to wrestle, but the sword was his specialty. Wrestling was a sport he hadn't worked at since his time with Royal. He grimaced. The thought of his ex-lover, who had betrayed him, was like a dash of cold water to his reeling senses. He would fight, if that was their wish. And he would win for his master.

He ran his hands over his oiled chest, feeling the ropes of muscles across his hard belly. Then he slicked back his long hair, twisting it into a braid, in the fashion he used to wear it before he was captured by the Kudites. Seeing his intent, Attlad pulled off a thong of leather from his wrist and tied it around the heavy blond braid. For a moment his fingers touched Micah's bicep. "Win for me," they signed against his warm skin, the words almost like a whisper in his ear, a secret that no one else could share.

Micah nodded, but he wasn't looking at Attlad. He was watching the open door where his opponent had just that moment appeared. He drew in his breath sharply.

Although Dalet's man was also naked, he was obviously not a sex slave. There was no gold chain with a disk suspended from rings in his nipples, nor did he wear the distinctive glittering red tear drop suspended from one ear. He didn't look like the usual Kudite male either. His skin was very dark and there was an olive green tinge to it that glinted ominously with flecks of gold in the flaring torchlight. He was shaved all over, his head his chest, his crotch. On his left bicep was a wide tattoo in the form of a linked chain. Micah had never seen anyone like him before.

The men gathered in a wide circle, laughing as they made wagers on the fighter of their choice. Micah couldn't tell from their gestures who the favourite was. He concentrated on his opponent, remembering the sword fight he had engaged in with Attlad when he was attacked without warning. Although some things were highly ritualized among the Kudites, fighting was always deadly serious and there were no rules that Micah had been able to decipher.

Cautiously he began to circle his opponent, trying to read his intentions in his eyes. He cursed the wine Attlad had poured down his throat, the food he had eaten from his master's hand. At least he had the energy from his unsatisfied cock. The old legend about no sex before battle had always seemed ridiculous before, but now he was aware of an edge, an energy moving from between his legs up and into his shoulders and arms. He knew he was hard, charged with the excitement of the fight. A quick glance at his opponent's crotch, told him that Dalet's man was aroused, his smooth glistening dark cock jutting out from between his legs. It also told him the man was a eunuch.

Shaken by the paradox of the man's heavy muscles, reasonably sized cock and lack of balls, Micah almost missed the slight narrowing of the eyes as his opponent attacked. He ducked, trying to go in under the man's guard, but there was no avoiding the long muscular arms entirely. The two men grappled together, sweat and oil dripping into Micah's eyes, obscuring his vision. Time after time he slid out of the arm locks and holds, but could never manage to gain any advantage to counterattack.   Then he realized the man had only been playing with him. Without warning. the dark giant grabbed Micah and slammed him to the ground. There was a gasp and a burst of laughter from the crowd of men who pressed closer as the victor pinned Micah to the floor, using his long hair and a knee to the throat. Gasping for air, Micah clawed at the man's eyes, then his groin, the only vulnerable point within reach. He grasped the hard dark cock and pulled. The man grimaced, his thin lips pulling back over his fine pointed teeth in a rictus of pain. Micah let go, then punched sharp and hard. In the instant the man lessened his grip, Micah arched his body, and flipped backwards out of reach. His victory was short lived, however, as the adversary knocked him off balance and instantly pinned him to the metal floor again. Micah could feel the vibration of the great ship through his whole body, thrumming inside his head as the hard knee thrust home into his throat. The room darkened around him and he sank into unconsciousness.

Micah opened his eyes with a gasp as ice cold water hit his naked body. As he struggled to deflect the torrent, he found his wrists and ankles were bound. He was on a sort of table, made of latticed strips of rawhide attached to a metal frame. Anger and frustration pounded through him as he twisted his wrists, the thongs cutting cruelly into his skin. Two men stood over him, their faces expressionless as they swabbed him down. They talked casually to each other, giving the impression not so much that they were exchanging opinions about his condition as if they were talking about something else entirely. Now and then, one of then laughed and looked at his co-worker for a moment, his face animated. Then he returned to his job, his hands moving over Micah's nakedness with utter disinterest, scrapping the oil off his skin, rubbing him down with a rough sponge. When they were finished with his front, they lowered a latticed platform similar to the one he was strapped to, switched his bounds and flipped his body as if he were so much meat. Then they went to work on his back.

Micah gritted his teeth as he lay spread-eagled, immobile on the frame, enduring their rough scraping. He was accustomed to handlers cleaning his body but he never got used to it. Perhaps, he thought wryly, he was annoyed by the impersonal aspect. In his limited experience, Kudite males were fascinated with his long blond hair and honey-brown skin. The women he hadn't met as yet. But these men were totally disinterested. There was nothing sexual in their touch, nothing personal at all. He might as well have been a draft horse, he thought with a stab of annoyance.

Besides their attitude, their ministrations were painful. Were they actually trying to draw blood, he wondered, pushing back the pain. Perhaps it was his punishment for losing the match. A wave of shame rolled over him as he remembered Attlad's fleeting touch, telling him to win. Even though the set-up of the whole match confused him, he had failed his master! There was no denying it.

From this position, he could see nothing but the metal floor and the boots of the men. Then he glimpsed a bare foot, very dark with a hint of olive green. He tensed. Nothing happened. Slowly he twisted his face to look up over his pinioned shoulder to where Dalet's slave stood watching. He grinned when he met Micah's stare, and raised his hand to sign;

"How have the mighty fallen!"

Micah stared at him in shock. Was it an accident that the signals translated to that familiar Terran quote? Or did this alien barbarian actually know he was quoting from the ancient Terran Bible? Since Micah's hands were securely tied, there was no chance to ask any questions. As he watched, the tall slave gave a final mocking salute, turned his back and sauntered over to the water jets, where he stood sluicing water over his magnificent body, his bald head gleaming in the bright light, the hard globes of his ass flexing.

Abruptly, the frame holding Micah tilted up and he was on his back again. The men now began pouring water over his head, washing his long hair. They paid no attention whatsoever about getting water or the harsh stinging soap in the slave's mouth or eyes, but kept up their bantering conversation as they continued their task, leaving Micah to cough and splutter, screwing his eyes tightly shut against the assault. When they were finished, they wrung his hair out, not caring about the pain as they combed it through their fingers, taking an interest for the first time in the long blond hair.

When he opened his eyes, they were making some adjustments to the frame. Abruptly, the upper side section seemed to slide into the lower section, with the result that his knees bent sharply, leaving his genitals and asshole utterly exposed. To his shame, he saw the eunuch slave was still watching, one dark hand stroking his gleaming tool that projected straight out from between his legs, obscene without the weight of balls at its base. Micah felt the hot blush of shame sweep up across his shaved chest. He could-n't read the intense expression on the dark face. Were those black eyes mocking him? Or was it lust that glowed for a moment in their depths? He turned his head away just in time to see a smooth hard object attached to a tube about to fed into his ass.

As the warm soapy water was forced inside him, he felt a strange euphoria. The table tilted backwards slightly, enough to let the solution deep inside him. Once more they chatted amiably between themselves, monitoring the flow of liquid with a casual glance. He could feel a rubber bulb inflating inside him, holding in the liquid but not slowing down the flow into his bowels. He tried to breath naturally, his eyes closed, floating with the erotic sensation of being filled, the pressure against his ass making his cock come to life. He tried not to think of his dark rival watching this, but even the thought of Dalet's slave did nothing to stop the erotic sensations from having their unwanted effect. Within moments, he was hard. He heard a groan escape from his tightly closed mouth. Another, this time a soft moan of pleasure.

The unease he had been feeling since coming to on the

table was gradually dissolving. Although he hadn't had quite this kind of water cleansing before, these men had done other similar things to him to prepare him for his master. This was merely more pleasant than he was used to.

Then the cramps hit. Involuntarily he clenched his fists against the onslaught of sudden pain. Noticing the movement, one of the attendant twisted a nob and the flow of liquid slowed, stopped. Then the dildo was withdrawn but the balloon apparently stayed in place, holding the water inside. The table tilted again, this time straight up till he was almost standing. They loosened his bound wrists, unlocked his ankle restraints, and he slid to the floor. One of the men slapped his scraped raw buttocks and pointed across the room to a narrow curving stool with a large bag suspended from it. Micah walked awkwardly, staggering now and then as the cramps hit him. All his concentration was on getting across the room to his destination. He felt a rubber tube of some sort hanging from his anus, but at this point he didn't care.

When he arrived at the stool, he saw it was only a frame to hold the bag. It was obvious what they expected of him. He straddled the contraption, feeling awkward and vulnerable as he squatted above the suspended bag. One of the men yanked on the rubber tube hanging from his hole and the water gushed out of him in bursts. Because he had so recently eaten, the procedure was repeated so many times, Micah lost count. In between times, they made him walk around the room, the water sloshing and gurgling inside him, pressing on his internal organs sometimes in a pleasant way, sometimes very painful. Then on a signal, he would squat over the stool and the plug would be yanked out, releasing the liquid. He was lightheaded by the time they were satisfied.

Next they attached wrist and ankle bracelets of heavy

brass, ornamented with blue symbols. They put a wide collar of similar design around his neck. It hung low, almost like an ornate necklace, he thought dizzily. Next, they lashed him to a chair while they brushed his hair and worked tiny blue and brass beads into the locks of hair in a pattern close to his head. A blue band was painted high on his forehead. Then they pulled him to his feet and motioned him to walk.

It's just that I'm being prepared for Attlad's pleasure, he told himself as he stumbled through the narrow ship's corridor after the handlers. But somehow he couldn't believe this comforting thought. A disturbing parallel had presented itself to his brain and refused to go away; the first time he had gone through a similar ritual, he had been sold as a sex slave and branded by his owner. Would Attlad consider selling him? Because he had let him down and lost the match? Or was his ownership what had been at stake all along? A cold shiver of fear jolted through him at the thought.

He was surprised to find he was back in the large circular room with the round table. At first glance, it was deserted. The brazier in the centre of the table had been extinguished, the coals glowing a sinister crimson. As his eyes adjusted to the dimness, he saw Attlad standing at the far side of the circle, holding a coloured skein of knotted leather thongs, which he recognized as some kind of ritual communication. For some reason, he felt these knots, which Attlad's fingers kept adding to as he watched, were tightly bound up with his future.

When the handlers withdrew, Micah moved towards his master. He had so many questions and yet was almost afraid to ask. Lit from beneath, Attlad's dark rugged face looked more like a cruel unreadable mask than the master he had given up so much to serve. His first impulse was to kneel at his feet and ask forgiveness for failing. But his soldier's pride intervened. The contest had been unfair. Surely Attlad had not expected him to win against a completely sober, well trained wrestler?

Then Attlad raised his head and looked at him. For a moment, it was as if his master's eyes had been replaced by two burning coals from the brazier. Micah almost stepped back in shock. Attlad flung the knotted twin on the metal table and signed furiously:

"You have disgraced me, Chento! I have lost more than you will ever know because of this!"

"But master, there was no way I could win in that situation! If you knew I was to fight, why did you pour wine down my—"

"You dare to question me?" Attlad knocked Micah's hands away angrily. Picking up a metal clip from the table, he grabbed Micah's wrist bracelets and attached them roughly to the ring that hung low on his gold and blue collar. Not being able to use his hands was a most effective gag. Micah could do nothing but stand there and simmer in his own anger. With another quick movement, Attlad attached a short chain between his ankle bracelets.

When he stood up again, Attlad began to shout at him, and although the exact meaning of the words was beyond Micah, the content was clear enough.

"This is grossly unfair," Micah shouted back, feeling better to get the words out even though Attlad had no idea what he was saying. "I am a Nebula Warrior —"

That phrase must have registered, because Attlad slapped him hard right across the face, almost knocking him over in his weakened state.

"God damn it, Attlad!" shouted Micah. "I love you! How can—"

Another slap, and this time Micah fell hard to one knee. When he raised his head, he saw an ornate long chest on the floor not three feet in front of him. The corners were carved and ornamented with brass animal heads, all with collars made of the glowing blue stones the Kudites were so fond of. The top was painted with symbols, one of which looked faintly familiar, but in his present state of anger and distress, he couldn't remember where he had seen it before.

As he struggled to rise to his feet, Attlad went to the box and opened it. He took something from inside and came back to Micah, gesturing for him to bend over. Micah obeyed, although it was awkward with his hands not free. With his forehead on the hard metal floor, his knees wide apart, he presented his ass for Attlad's inspection. Attlad touched his ass cheeks, his hands resting against the muscular globes for a moment, then one hand skid down the crack and opened his ass hole. The other hand thrust what felt like a damp hard ball up his anus. Micah caught his breath, trying to prepare for more pain, when it suddenly stopped. His sphincter muscles closed around a rubber tube of some kind. The ball was still inside, and he could feel another smaller ball protruding from his ass. Attlad squeezed this and at once Micah felt a cool liquid released inside him. There was a slight stinging sensation, then it stopped.

Attlad clapped his hands, a familiar signal for him to get up. Then his master motioned him to the chest and pointed. Micah looked down and saw that the inside of the box was hollowed out in the shape of a man about his size. He looked back at Attlad, sure he must have misunderstood the signal, but his master pointed again, this time pushing him firmly on the back. There was no mistaking the intention. He was to get into this box, this coffin, and.... What? Would he suffocate? Would he be sent back to Earth Base Gamma, a rejected slave? Would....

Micah swayed, his head suddenly fuzzy. He felt Attlad's strong arms guiding him, lifting him down into the chest, fitting his legs into the place hollowed out for them.

"Attlad..." Micah could barely see, now, and panic swooped into his clouded mind. "What's happening to me?"

Were those tears on his master's face? Micah blinked, trying to see more clearly. Attlad laid the knotted leather thongs on his stomach and attached one end around the base of his cock. Even this Micah could barely feel, though he had seen the knot pulled tight around his flesh.

"I'm going to die," he thought in panic as the lid began to close over him. "Oh god! I'm going to die!"

TWO

icah opened his eyes to darkness and the feeling his whole universe was swaying. He tried to lift a hand to rub his eyes and found he couldn't move. His sluggish mind refused to process what was happening. Even remembering the events just prior to his blacking out proved a problem. He lay there, stunned, inert, letting sensations roll over him; velvet darkness, the soft prickle of heat, the slight syncopation of his own heart beat pulsing gently under his skin. The scent of roses oozing from the warm wood, touched his nakedness with invisible petals. It felt as if he was on a boat, the lake choppy as the wind whipped the waves into small mountains and valleys. His stomach lurched uneasily. He was hanging onto the gunwales as his father adjusted the jets of the boat's engines to try to take the rough water into account. Even so, the small craft swayed from side to side, but he knew he was safe. His father would get them back safely into port.... Micah blinked and tried to force his mind back to reality. Where would this craft take him? He doubted there would be a safe harbor waiting at the end of this unsettling journey.

There was a pattern cut into the wood above him, he noticed, small air holes in the shape of flower petals all along the top of the box that enclosed him. In one way, the feeling of being tightly surrounded by wood gave him a sense of security, safety, like when he was with his father all those years ago. The smooth sweet-smelling wood embraced his shoulders, his hips, the small of his back, almost as if the interior of the chest had been made from a mould of his body. His thighs, the calves of his legs, even his cock and balls, felt as if sealed in by another skin. Above his face there was a space of about a few inches, the hard surface so close that he could feel his own breath. There were enough tiny pinholes so he would not suffocate. Even here, the inner surface of the box followed the contours of his body. He knew that inside, the lid of the box was like a mask reflecting the planes and angles of his face. It gave him an odd feeling, as if part of him had been taken away and blended with the wood.

At last he realized he was being carried. Perhaps his brain was clearing from the confusing haze he woke up to. Had he been drugged somehow? He remembered the sudden weakness and confusion that came on after Attlad's ministrations. With a great effort of concentration, he tightened his sphincter muscles but could feel nothing but an odd coolness deep inside his ass. Were there drugs of some sort in the concoction that had been thrust deep into him? Pacifiers to keep him calm and docile while he was taken to ... wherever Attlad was sending him? A wave of despair washed over him, followed at once by a cold anger at the man who had so betrayed him! For a while, he had abandoned himself to his own inner fantasies, revelling in the role of a real slave to a powerful master. Caught up in the discovery of his own inner passions, he had forgotten the other side of the coin; to these people, he was a slave in a very real sense, an object to be dealt with and disposed of as his owner saw fit. So much for the perfect relationship he thought he had gained with Attlad! Well, the Kudites may have forgotten he was a Nebula Warrior, but he had not. They would be reminded, he would see to that! He found he was grinding his teeth so hard his head hurt. With an effort, he stopped himself and turned his thoughts to his present situation. If he was a slave, who was his owner?

He closed his eyes, forcing himself to concentrate on the lulling motion, refusing to indulge in thoughts of wild revenge or self-defeating rage. Not yet ... not yet. A good warrior bides his time. There would come a moment when he would find a way back to Attlad, and the former master would discover what it meant to betray the trust of a Nebula Warrior! For that to happen, he would have to be very careful. He would have to curb his temper and remember that he was still a slave. For now.

His closed-in world tilted abruptly, so that his feet were above his head. Stairs, he thought suddenly. We're going up a flight of stairs! The jouncing of the coffin-like chest confirmed this suspicion and for the first time, Micah realized they must be off the ship. They must have landed some time ago, while he was still unconscious. He felt the tension like a force outside himself, his still flaccid muscles unable to respond to the impulses from his slowly awakening brain. The Citadel! They had arrived at the fabled stronghold of the Kudites.

He had heard many veiled references to the place during his time at the Complex, and always there was that underlying uneasiness, that tinge of anxiety. He had the distinct feeling that no one wanted to come here, Attlad least of all, yet there was nothing clear to go on. All he knew for certain was that most of the women were here, a fact that didn't seem sinister in itself. He wished now he had tried to gain more information about the place, but no one had ever seemed eager to talk about it. Now, he supposed, he was about to find out why.

For awhile he had been aware of a dimming of the light coming in through the tiny air-holes. They must be indoors, he decided. The heat was building inside the confined space and sweat slicked his body. He could feel the perspiration covering his smooth oiled chest like a blanket under the gold and blue collar. His wrists in their heavy bracelets were also slick with sweat and the knotted message strings stuck to his belly and sensitive shaved crotch.

The swaying stopped. In spite of the air-holes, it was getting hard to breath. His heart hammered in his chest, beating in his ears. The box was lowered. With a soft thud, it hit the ground.

Nothing happened for a long time. He strained to hear what was going on outside, but little penetrated his sealed-in world. After the first few dull thuds and deep booming echoes, as if great doors were being slammed, it seemed as if he had been abandoned, left alone in his ornate sarcophagus. Panic fluttered in his chest for a moment, until years of training came to his rescue. He took deep breaths, narrowing the focus of his thoughts to slow the wild beating of his heart. Gradually his chest began to rise and fall, barely expanding as he sank into a near trance. In... out... slow... fade....

White light burst in his face like a grenade as the cover was removed. He winced, trying to turn his face away, without success. A dark shape outlined in brightness hovered over him for a moment. Then he heard the familiar liquid language, but he could separate no words from the flow. The voice was a woman's. The change in timbre was enough to confuse his imperfect ear for the language. Before he could assimilate this new information, his resting place began to tilt on end, until he was almost standing. Like an exhibit in an ancient museum, he thought wryly. Ahead of him stretched a great marble hall, lined with rough-hewn pillars of bright red rock. He had no time to notice any details before a naked youth stepped in front of him. He wore nothing but a ring of blue and silver stones encircling his stubby cock, which made it stick out in front of his shaved crotch like a jewelled knob. He was totally hairless, except for the very top of his head where his black hair had been braided into the tresses of a long narrow leather thong that hung down his back. His features were soft and delicate, vulnerable as a young girl, his eyebrows plucked into fine, questioning arches. A gold chain decorated with pearls hung low on his narrow hips.

Micah was so focussed on the boy, he didn't see the woman until she stood directly in front of him. She was taller than the boy, her luxuriant reddish brown hair falling over one shoulder in a thick braid. Blue stones and tiny silver and gold beads were braided close to her head. Just like his own hair, he realized, with a jolt, but she had no blue band painted on her forehead. Her skin was milk white, as if she rarely had reason to go outside the luxurious rooms of what seemed to be some kind of palace. She wore a soft flowing robe of some diaphanous material, cinched in at the waist with a black sash that looked as if woven from human hair. Her large grey eyes regarded Micah cooly, assessing her new possession from head to toe, coming back to rest on his broad shoulders, his muscular thighs, his cock, still bound to the knotted message strings.

Micah blushed under the detached appraisal. When she reached out and touched his cock, it was all he could do to restrain his anger from betraying him into useless pulling against the clips that fastened his bracelets to his collar.

Micah felt the heat of embarrassment stain his chest and face a bright red as her soft hand trailed over his naked crotch, the fingers pushing under his cock to the shaved balls. He felt himself stir at her touch, in spite of his efforts to remain detached. Then she paused, and traced part of the tattooed dragon on his stiffening shaft. Attlad's emblem, his unalterable mark. The sight of it seemed to annoy her and with an impatient shake of her head, she motioned to the boy to untie the message strings knotted around the head of his cock.

The boy's touch was firm, efficient as he untied the knots, yet Micah felt a distinct caress before the slave handed the ceremonial message to the woman with a bow of his head. As he turned, Micah saw an angry red welt slicing across his pale buttocks. The leather thong braided into his hair hung below the crack in his small tight little ass.

Abruptly, the woman signed for him to step out of the box. Micah almost missed the command signal, so fascinated was he with the strange compelling beauty of the boy. Obediently, he forced his stiff joints to function and moved awkwardly from his place. But he had been immobile a long time and as his bare feet touched the cool marble floor, he lost his balance and fell heavily to his knees.

The woman's laugh rang out like bells above him as she stepped forward and undid the clasp holding his hands to his collar.

"Stand up," she signalled.

Micah obeyed and stood at ease, swaying slightly, hands behind his back, legs apart. It was a posture that now came to him quite naturally. He noticed a small blue gryphon embroidered into the material on her left shoulder. Although its stance and colour were quite different from the dragon symbol tattooed on his cock, it still reminded him of his former master, but this time the anger steadied him.

The woman began to walk around him, her head tilted slightly to the right as she studied her new property. She murmured softly to herself as the boy looked on with interest, his dark eyes not missing anything. Micah felt her hand cup his ass cheek, her fingers dig into his biceps, a long nail scratch against his nipples. She tugged at the gold chain linking the rings in his tits. Micah stared straight ahead, refusing to consider what she might have in store for him. He would endure a great deal. He could get through this, whatever it might be. Somehow, some way, he would get back to Attlad and the man would learn what it meant to betray a Nebula Warrior.

She took handfuls of his long blond hair and ran it through her fingers. "No man should be allowed to have hair so beautiful," she signed. She gave his hair one last painful tug and turned away. Her inspection finished, she threw an order at the boy without glancing at him. At once, he ran off to do her bidding.

The woman sat down on a curved marble bench beside what looked like a cabinet. She drummed her long pearlized blue nails against the hard surface as she studied him consideringly.

"You are an interesting physical specimen," she said, her pale hands moving languidly as she signed the words. "I am impressed with Attlad for sending such a gift. He must have enjoyed you a great deal. You are not exactly to my taste, but I'm sure my friends and I will find much amusement with you." She smiled and ran her tongue over her red shiny lips. "You were a warrior, I am told."

"Yes..." He hesitated, not sure of the form of address.

"You may call me Lady. You will have no use for all those muscles now. Perhaps we can slim you down a bit. You will find life much less strenuous here, in some ways." Again she smiled, but there was little warmth in the expression.

The boy returned and stood in front of her, carrying a pale pink garment folded over one arm. In the other, he held a gold chain, decorated with small pearls. The woman nodded at him.

"Put the tunic on him," she signed. "You, Chento, kneel so he can reach you better. You are not a boy, to go naked in public in the women's quarters."

Micah did as he was told and the boy turned towards him. He smiled shyly, his beautiful face losing the look of fragile sadness for a few moments, as his hand touched Micah and signed quickly. "I'm sorry to have to do this," the movements said. "I have no choice." Micah dared not acknowledge the message. He watched the boy's smile fade as he began to arrange the almost sheer fabric over Micah's head and shoulders. The tunic fell to just below his ass cheeks, barely covering his cock. Then the boy fitted the pearl chain around Micah's waist so that it hung loosely at his hips. He fastened the ends with the small hand tool, welding the links together permanently. There was no way to take the belt off now.

The woman nodded with satisfaction and signed to Micah to stand up. He felt even more exposed than when he had been completely naked before her. The flimsy garment seemed designed to reveal more than it hid. It was cut low in the front to show his nipples with their gold rings. There were no sleeves and the armholes were so loose, the garment barely came together at his waist before separating again in a slit that revealed most of his thigh. It made him feel obscene.

The woman got up and took the boy's long pigtail in one hand. With the other, she reached under Micah's short skirt and grasped his cock, her thumb finding the tiny gold ring Attlad had put there. There was a small clip at the end of the braid and this she slid into the ring, fastening his cock to the boy's hair.

"I expect you've been trained well enough to know not to touch yourself, or the boy," she signed. Micah nodded, his jaw tense. "Bar, take him to the pool."

She watched as the boy turned obediently and started down the long room. Micah soon found his cock pulled painfully no matter how he tried to match the boy's shorter stride. It was hard not to stumble, having to keep so close, yet not allowed to touch. The boy's dimpled ass cheeks rose and fell as he walked. Micah could feel the heat from his flushed naked skin. His own skin felt hot with shame to be paraded like this. The thin garment was sticking to the crack in his ass, but he was afraid to pull it free. The woman walked beside them, watching with a smile of pleasure at his obvious discomfort.

They walked like this through a great marble gateway, along a corridor to an enclosed garden. A turquoise pool rippled in the mottled sunlight that shone through a latticed roof, thick with vines. A throng of girls lay about on long couches, wrapped in colourful sarongs or swam nearly naked in the pool. There were a few boys like Bar, their stubby cocks ornamented with the blue and silver beads. One had a sort of silver cage over the red knob of the shaft. On closer inspection, Micah saw his arms were tied to a tree, his long braid wrapped around the trunk keeping his head tilted back at an unnatural angle. Tears slid down his cheeks.

"Girls, here is my new pet Chento, a bond gift from Attlad to mark our agreement."

There was a chorus of interested comments from the girls, who flocked around him, their hands in his hair, under his tunic, tugging at the rings in his nipples.

One girl said something to his lady, who laughed and turned to Micah. "She says it gives her pleasure to see a man's nipples standing at attention, like a young girl's at the touch of her lover's lips." She reached up and flicked his right tit with a long blue nail. "Bar, serve the ladies their drinks, now."

At once Bar went to the table under the tree by the bound boy, Micah forced to follow him closely. He felt even more awkward with all these eyes following him, laughing at his ungainly predicament. He didn't know what to do with his hands. Bar hastily filled a tray with tall glass of some clear green liquid and started to serve the girls, who had returned to their couches. As he bent his head to hand them the drinks, Micah's cock was pulled unmercifully forward. He gritted his teeth and tried not to see the sly looks or react to the hands that slid under his tunic to feel his shaved crotch and balls. They were used to boys, and apparently a full grown man to fondle was a special treat.

Finally they tired of this sport and he was unclipped from Bar's hair. He stood beside his lady's couch, watching her eat and drink and realized how very hungry he was. He had lost track of the time, but his stomach apparently had not and now began to make loud noises of complaint.

"I think it's feeding time for your pets," one of the girls signed, laughing. "I think the new one has been eyeing Bar quite hungrily. Perhaps you should feed the boy to him?"

"Excellent idea. Get him ready while I take a swim with this one." She reached up and casually undid the clasps holding his tunic to his shoulders. It fell to his waist. With a grunt of annoyance she pulled it though the loose girdle of pearls and Micah was naked again. She pointed to the pool, then took off her own long robe, revealing a twist of cloth coming up from between her legs to cover her small breasts.

Micah walked beside her down the steps into the soothing water, unsure what he we was supposed to do. He watched her immerse herself and when she started to swim, he followed along beside her. She made no protest and at last he began to relax. In spite of the difficulty caused by the heavy bracelets on his wrists and ankles, he was enjoying the water, the sun, the mild exercise. Perhaps she had had her fun for awhile.

Then he felt her grasp his hair and hit his ass with her hand. He began to swim in earnest, pulling her after him, attached to his hair. When he got to the end, he paused, only to feel the sting of her small hand again on his ass. At once he turned around and swam back as fast as he could, this time barely pausing before turning about. He lost count of the laps he did, dragging her along, artfully tangled in his long hair, his scalp screaming in protest, until at last she called a halt to her fun.

It was the pain that made him out of breath. His chest was heaving as he walked back up the steps to the courtyard. He almost stumbled when he saw what was spread out for his meal. The naked boy lay on his back, his hands tied to his ankles with silk scarves so that his knees were pulled back sharply. Every orifice was stuffed with some delicacy; his mouth held what looked like a puffed pastry, brimming over with cream filling, his belly button cradled a miniature apple, chunks of meat dripping with gravy hung from his distended anus. Held precariously between his knees was a large succulent tuber of some kind, drizzled with butter. Long green beans were woven in a circle around his stubby little cock, now bare of the blue jewels and painted with what looked like thick red wine. His whole body had been dribbled with some fragrant deep brown sauce, which held small slices of carrots and other vegetables Micah didn't recognize stuck in place on the boy's body.

He could feel all eyes on him, watching his reaction with amusement. In spite of his shock, his stomach growled as the rich heady smell of the food assailed his nostrils, and his mouth began to water in anticipation. Blushing, he glanced at his lady for instructions.

"I knew you were hungry for the boy, weren't you?" she asked, and even her hands seemed to be laughing at him as they made the signs.

"I am hungry, yes."

"I can see that," she said, looking pointedly as his half erect cock. "Eat, but don't touch the boy with your hands. Understand?"

"Yes, lady."

"Just to make sure you don't forget, put your hands behind your back." She gestured to one of the girls who came over with a brightly coloured scarf. They fastened the scarf to his wrist bracelets, chattering and laughing among themselves as they did so. Then he felt a slap on his bare ass and a slight push sent him towards the helpless Bar.

He knelt between the boy's raised knees and reached carefully for the brimming yellow-gold food, piled so temptingly in its hard bowl-shaped skin. As he bit into it, his mouth was filled with the spicy goodness of sweet potato, squash and onions, all seemingly in the one vegetable. He scooped the meaty food out of its shell with his tongue, wolfed it down and then took the husk in his teeth and laid it beside Bar on the couch. He felt a bit of the tension go out of the boy's legs, now he no longer had to hold anything between his knees.

The taste of food had only sharpened Micah's appetite. He could hardly remember the last time he had eaten. All thoughts of his humiliating position, his concern for the boy, the women watching him in amusement, were gone as he crouched lower and fastened his teeth in the small chunk of meat protruding from the glistening distended mouth of the boy's anus. As he pulled and chewed through the meat, another chunk appeared in its place. Pausing, Micah pulled back on the meat and realized the boy had been stuffed with a whole string of bite-sized morsels, threaded together. The food was still warm and gravy oozed out between the boy's greasy ass-cheeks, forming a small puddle on the marble bench. Micah thrust his tongue inside and sucked out cube after cube. Still hungry, he chewed the last piece of meat and licked up the gravy that had dripped onto the marble. Raising his head, he munched thorough the green beans and took the small stub of a cock in his mouth, sucking at the hot sauce it was painted with. It was as if he had lost track of the difference between the boy and the food his body was providing. He felt the boy react, the cock hard and pulsing under his tongue. But it was a surprise when the little penis erupted, filling his mouth with thick come. Even this fluid was flavoured with the hot spices that still coated the cock. Micah swallowed, sobered a little by the trembling of the slender boy he feasted on so callously. Gently, he licked the cock clean and moved up to the take the apple from the boy's navel. As he chewed the fruit, he looked at Bar for the first time, seeing the partially shaved head, the distended tits, the delicate collar bones. The wide dark eyes were glazed with tears. Micah felt desire flood his body with heat. He took the pastry from the boy's mouth, sucked up the cream filling, chewed the flaky shell. He pressed his mouth against Bar's, licking the rest of the sugar from his parted lips. He felt Bar's tongue in his mouth before he was pulled back. He glanced over his shoulder.

"Enough play." Her hands were sharp and quick in shaping their words. "You want him. Take him now."

Micah looked back at the boy, his slender vulnerability, the big dark eyes staring into his. He looked down at the little cock he could still taste in his mouth, its taste so mingled with spice and pastry and meat it was part of it. Food. Something he needed, craved. Now that he looked at it more closely, he realized the cock had been surgically altered, chopped off below the head. Micah swallowed. Someone untied his wrists and he stood up, moving between the boy's knees. He grasped his narrow hips and pulled him closer. He rolled the bound legs back to expose the greasy asshole. It was still spilling gravy and Micah pushed his hard cock into the tight warmth suddenly overcome with lust. The boy began to shake as Micah pushed further inside, but by now he couldn't restrain himself and slammed all the way until his shaved balls hit that smooth gravy-smeared ass. Bar let out a small scream, but Micah couldn't hear anything but the rush of blood in his ears as he climaxed and shot deep into the boy's bowels. With a heaving chest, he pulled out and stood panting, eyes unfocused.

It was his new 'master' who led him to the other end of the bench and ordered the boy to clean him off. He was still shaking as Bar took him in his mouth and sucked him clean. As he stood in the courtyard, his cock in the boys mouth, several of the girls turned away from the scene with an expression of disgust. Micah watched them go to the pool and sit on the steps, chatting together. It didn't seem to be real, he thought. It was like a scene out of some story disk back home.

A wonderful languor drifted over him. He felt drenched in sun, sex, food. He smiled to himself.

Then he saw the man standing in the doorway watching him.

"Attlad," he breathed.

THREE

o, Dadani, this is the famous gift." The man signed as he spoke, obviously for Micah's benefit. He stared at the Terran, his dark grey eyes hard and shiny like pebbles. Then he laughed, his hands going to his hips as he swayed back and forth in exaggerated mirth. "My brother has strange tastes, but then I always knew that."

"He is different," she replied, looking at Micah coolly. "He will prove amusing."

"You'd better get him cleaned up for the banquet. You don't want to disgust our guests."

She turned immediately and signed to a house-slave who had been standing nearby. "Clean them."

At once, he untied the boy and pulled him roughly to his feet. With practised ease, he undid the bracelets on Micah's wrists and ankles. Then he led the way to the other end of the courtyard where a stream of water gushed out of the rock above their heads, and thrust Micah and Bar under the warm cascade.

"Clean yourselves thoroughly," he signed and flung a

large rough sponge at each of them.

Under his watchful eye, Micah began to rub his face, his shoulders, his chest, his bracelets, relieved to have the chance to rinse off all traces of his recent meal. He was careful not to touch his genitals, but a quick glance at Bar showed that he had not been so cautious. One small hand surreptitiously rubbed his truncated cock, his expression making it plain that the spices still stung unbearably. At once Micah moved closer in an effort to shield him, but it was too late. A shout behind him showed that Kerdas, too, had been watching and had caught sight of the forbidden act. Bar cringed as Kerdas strode towards them.

"Out!" he signed imperiously.

At once they both stepped out from under the waterfall, dripping on the smooth flagstones.

Bar fell to his knees. "Forgive me," he signed, mouthing silent words in a desperate plea. "I only tried to wash away the fire. There was no pleasure for me, lord! None!"

Micah watched Kerdas's cruel face, those features so like Attlad and yet so different. His brother, had he understood the signs right? There was something about this man that made him very fearful. If he was to have a say in his life from now on, he knew he was in for a lot of pain and grief. This man had the look of a sadist about his eyes, and yet, when he turned his head just that way ....

"Kerdas, the boy meant no disrespect," Dadani said, and she, too was signing. "He was merely forgetful."

"Dadani, you are too soft with the pearlboys. That's why you agreed to let me discipline them, no? He must learn what it means to forget!"

Dadani shrugged and walked away.

Kerdas reached down and grasped the thin pigtail at the top of Bar's shaven head and twisted the clip that held it in place. The long thin leather strands braided in with his own hair came away, becoming in that instant a cruel whip.

"Inside." He pointed to the door and Bar got to his feet. The wet naked boy burst into hopeless tears as he left the courtyard in front of Kerdas. Almost at once, his screams split the air. No one payed the slightest attention as they went on chattering and laughing amongst themselves.

The sun had dried Micah, now. Only his long hair was still damp and the slave who had been watching him, now dried that with a rough towel. Then he was dressed in a tunic, which another house slave had brought, this one a pale yellow, that came halfway down his bare thighs. It, too, was cut low in front to show off his nipples, the rings and the chain connecting them that glinted in the sun. The pearl and gold girdle was still in place low on his hips. Strangely enough, this unfamiliar touch of luxury made him feel awkward and vaguely ashamed.

The girls began leaving the courtyard in groups of two or three. Several house-slaves entered and started to clean away the debris from his `lunch'. The screams from Bar had stopped and an eerie silence beat against his ears. He swallowed.

"Come." Dadani walked quickly inside and made her way through the large marble chamber where he had first arrived in what he now thought of wryly as his `gift box'. Draped over one of the black marble benches, was the pale whipped body of Bar, his sobs muffled by the handful of Kerdas's tunic thrust into his mouth. Kerdas stood nearby, stripped to the waist, drinking a goblet of wine. Sweat clung to his tanned muscular chest and the sight of him sent a sharp twinge of desire through Micah, in spite of the circumstances. Ashamed at this reaction, he looked away. Dadani exchanged a few words with Kerdas, never even glancing at the naked boy. Then she waved and left the room.

Micah followed her through a series of narrow corridors, dimly lit by a strip of yellow light running along the middle of the ceiling. A low hum seemed to emanate from the walls on either side, but Micah couldn't pin down the source. Dadani opened a door and went through to a series of small rooms, hung with panels of brightly coloured painted silk. In the last room, he caught sight of a large bed, covered with a red canopy.

Dadani was already shedding her cloths as she walked, as unmindful of his presence as if he weren't there at all. He bent down and picked up the gown she had walked out of and held it awkwardly, smelling the heady perfume that wafted up from the soft material. She beckoned and he followed her into the bed chamber.

She took off the last strip of damp cloth, letting it fall to the floor. She lay back among the pillows and smiled up at him, her lush naked body glowing like a pearl against the dark red coverlet. He stood beside her, uncertain what was expected of him. Casually, she reached out under his tunic and fondled his cock.

"I don't suppose you got much chance to use that with Attlad," she said, her hands forming the signs with languid elegance.

He blushed, not sure what he was supposed to say. What did she mean by the term `use'?

She smiled, seeing his discomfort, and tugged at his cock again. His sensitive penis responded at once, increasing Micah's embarrassment. "Perhaps you will provide more amusement than I expected," she said, raising a silken eyebrow. "But not until you are docked, as is only proper for one of my sex slaves."

"I do not understand the term," Micah said, his hands hesitating as he formed the words. He had a sudden vivid picture of Bar's red mutilated cock; too short, too blunt, his balls hard and unnatural. A terrible suspicion sent a chill of fear through him.

She looked up at him with a puzzled frown. "You don't need to understand, Chento," she said airily, and got to her feet.

He watched her choose a new robe from a cupboard crammed with bright colour. She twisted her hair in a pile high on her head, one part cascading in a long braid decorated with coloured beads. She hummed to herself as she did all this, then came to him and sprayed him liberally with her perfume.

"I want everyone to identify you as mine, even by the scent," she said. For the first time, her smile touched her lovely brown eyes.

Kerdas came in at that moment and looked at Dadani admiringly. He wore a soft leather tunic, unlaced to show a good part of his chest. He touched her luxuriant dark hair and murmured something. When he glanced at Micah, all tenderness vanished.

Micah tensed, seeing the flinty eyes assess his filmy garment. Then Kerdas smiled, a most unpleasant expression on his face. "His ugly cock is too prominent, Dadani," he signed. "I'll tie it up out of the way, so you are not embarrassed by his alien crudity. My brother may like such things, but no lady could be expected to share his base pleasure."

She shrugged. "As you wish, Kerdas. All that will be attended to later anyway."

"Good, but for now, this will do." He pulled the leather laces from his tunic and grabbed Micah's cock. With deft fingers, he tied one end around the stiffening head. In spite of how Micah felt about the man intellectually, his body continued to betray him, his cock lengthening, thickening under the man's hand. Kerdas set his jaw and walked around Micah. He reached through the slave's legs, grabbed the leather lace and pulled it back sharply. Micah bit back a cry as his cock was twisted out of shape. Kerdas ripped the material of Micah's scant garment to allow him to tie the other end of the lace around the low-hanging beaded girdle. This done, he walked back in front of Micah and pulled up the front of the tunic. Nothing was revealed but the shaved pubic area. There was no sign of a cock, no sign of Attlad's dragon tattooed on its length.

Micah tried to work the pain through his body, tried to deal with the insulting implication of emasculation that the simple diabolical act had accomplished. Dadani reached out an inquisitive hand and ran a sharp fingernail over his sensitive shaved crotch.

"Very nice," she said. "We'll keep him like that till the docking is accomplished. Come. It's time."

It was a long painful walk for Micah, following behind his two tormenters to the banquet place. He kept his legs apart, which made it slightly easier to walk. He felt the draft on his ass as the two halves of the torn tunic separated, baring his cheeks. The thin rawhide cut into his crack rubbing against his asshole. It was amazing that the simple act of walking should now take all his concentration.

The banquet hall was entered through another court-yard, surrounded by towering cliff-like structures that almost disappeared above them. Their steps echoed in the man made canyons of stone and then they were inside the large dark hall. These walls, too, were covered with silken hangings, much finer than what Micah was used to seeing back at the Complex. A curved table ran all around the periphery of the place and half-naked servers of both genders rushed to keep the wine glasses and large platters filled with every manner of delicacy.

Micah kept close to Dadani, who was greeted with cries of pleasure from everyone. They were all curious about him, too, some of them even coming over to inspect him close up. Even the young women were quick to feel his pectorals, slide a soft hand under his ass. There was much laughter when one man held up the tunic to reveal his sexless crotch.

"Not much good in bed this one," one man signed, his hands shaking with his laughter.

"What kind of a soldier could he have been without a spear?" laughed another wit.

"Quite a change from Bar and his kind," a woman remarked, her eyes running over his broad shoulders. "If you don't want him...."

Dadani laughed as she sat down at her place. "I'll keep him, thank you. He was a gift, after all. It's not polite to hand on a gift." She looked around the curve of the table and inclined her head graciously.

Following her gaze, Micah felt himself go scarlet. Attlad sat there, watching, one hand on the shaved head of a kneeling boy. His intense steel grey eyes looked only at Dadani, acknowledging her remark with a dignified nod. Then he turned back to the boy, pushing the shaved head down under the table, between his knees.

Micah swallowed, his anger so palpable it threatened to chock him. Then he saw the greenish-brown eunuch wrestler who had won the match sitting further along at the table and for a moment, he thought he would pass out with repressed fury. The man was watching him, an amused expression on his arresting dark face. A tug on Micah's tunic, brought him quickly to a sense of what was expected from him. He looked back at his new owner.

"Pay attention!" She frowned.

"I will give him something to focus on," Kerdas said with a grin. He grabbed a small carafe from the table, spun Micah around, pulled up his tunic at the back and poured liquid down the crack of his ass onto the engorged head of his cock. Then he slapped one cheek hard and turned him around again. "Now you will remember where you are and who you belong to," he said.

Micah clenched his hands as the cool liquid began to glow hotter and hotter, until he felt as if his cock was on fire. Stabbing flames licked long the painfully twisted penis. He began to tremble.

"Walk around the whole circle of the table, so everyone can admire my new present," Dadani ordered. "Here. Kneel and take a drink from me first. Then you will kneel beside each guest and take what they offer you. Kudites at the Citadel know how to welcome strangers, even disobedient alien slaves."

He knelt beside her and opened his mouth as she tipped the wine for him to drink. He knew better than to touch the goblet. Then he moved to the next guest, then the next, his head reeling with the pain from his cock and the effort to keep as much dignity as possible. After a while, the dark laughing faces swam before him. One young woman wiped the tears from his eyes with the corner of her robe and kissed his wine stained lips. Another held a handful of his blond hair to her face and inhaled its scent. Several of the men ran one hand under his tunic as he drank, fondling his shaven balls and stretched cock.

And then he came to Attlad. Blinking back the tears of humiliation and pain, he knelt beside the master who had betrayed him. Attlad held out the cup and Micah opened his lips. As he drank, he glared into those steel grey eyes, which stared back at him, giving nothing away. He was aware of the boy crouching between Attlad's knees, aware of his own burning cock that hurt even more in its efforts to grow hard. He swallowed the strong red wine in great gulps, as if the cool liquid could douse the fire between his legs. Attlad tipped the cup further... further. Micah gulped noisily, trying to keep up, but the liquid spilled out over his chin, staining his bare chest and the delicate fabric of his scanty tunic. Micah laid his right hand on Attlad's thigh under the table and made the sign, "Why?" Abruptly, Attlad pulled the cup back and turned away.

Micah set his jaw in anger, got painfully to his feet and moved to the man beside Attlad. This man spilled even more wine down Micah's throat, apparently inspired by Attlad's example, then motioned to his slave to come and lick off what had spilled. Micah endured in silence as a nameless, faceless boy licked his skin clean of the spilled wine. When the boy was pulled away, Micah got to his feet and continued the humiliating ritual, until he came to the wrestler. This man was a slave too, and yet he was sitting here as a guest. Was he expected to kneel to him? As he hesitated, the man looked up at him and grinned, holding out the goblet. Aware that Kerdas and Dadani were both watching, Micah knelt and accepted the cup. Surprisingly, the man tilted the goblet only enough to wet his lips, then withdrew it.

He laid his other hand on Micah's shoulder. "Even this shall pass," he signed with a smile.

Stunned, Micah stared back at him. He opened his mouth, saw a warning in the black eyes and closed it again.

"Shit," he muttered as he struggled to his feet.

By the time he reached Dadani, he stank from the spilled drink and slobber and was lightheaded with pain and all the wine he had been forced to drink. He sank down on the floor beside her, trying to get relief by rubbing his burning cock against the cool tiles of the floor. Absently, she handed him a cube of fruit. When he reached out for it, she slapped his hand away and thrust it between his lips.

The barbaric feasting went on and on. Dadani sent a house slave to bring back one of her favourite boys, who arrived, dressed in a white embroidered tunic, his face pale, his wrists and ankles bearing the marks of restraints. He sat on the wide bench beside her, leaning his head meekly against her breast while she fed him tidbits and talked to the woman beside her.

A platform in the middle of the circular table rose up through the floor to a blast of trumpets and a group of half-naked dancers appeared. The girls wore long filmy garments decorated with tiny mirrors, through which their painted pierced nipples were clearly visible. The boys were bare chested, their tunics cut away to display their painted blue nipples, pierced with large silver rings. Brass bells and small hollow rattles hung from these rings. The obvious weight of these baubles stretched the nipples considerably, causing strained expressions on the boys' faces. They had the partly shaved heads of the slave boys Micah was beginning to identify as belonging to the women, and they wore jewelled girdles similar to his slung low on their hips. The girls had long flowing hair and, like the boys, were naked under all the gossamer.

Wild cheers greeted their appearance. By now a great deal of wine and ale had been consumed, and the faces around the large table were flushed. Quite a few of the company had already left, apparently having no desire to witness the uninhibited revelry they knew was to come. The atmosphere had become even freer as the voices grew loud and demanding. Kerdas reached up and pulled one of the girl dancers down on his knee. He pushed back the filmy covering and buried his head between her lush breasts. Dadani slapped at him playfully and laughed.

Micah watched the sensuous display and felt the ache in his groin become almost unbearable. It wasn't the willowy boys who turned him on but the hot sweaty men who reached for them, pawing at their bejewelled crotches, pinching the round globes of their asses. Some they pulled across the table and into their laps, as Kerdas had done with the girl, and after a while there were no dancers left to entertain.

Next, two of the men climbed into the platform left vacant by the dancers and pulled off their tunics. At once they began to wrestle. It was a good-natured fight and neither one was in any shape to acquit themselves well. Nevertheless, the whole table galvanized and took sides, cheering on the favourite. When both men had fallen to the floor too exhausted to continue, it appeared to be a draw and their friends pulled them back to their places.

Kerdas jumped to his feet and shouted to the assembled group. He waved his hands, signing so all could understand.

"Our alien slave is obviously turned on by all the fun. Who can give him release?"

Shouts filled the air at once and Micah was pulled to his feet. Dazed, he climbed onto the table, as he was told and stumbled to the centre space. Kerdas climbed after him and yanked Micah's tunic off, revealing his sexless crotch to gales of laughter from the assembled group.

"Such a man needs a special sex partner," Kerdas signed. "A true sex machine to satisfy his alien lust!"

At once a shout went up, several names shouted over and over. Micah felt his head throb with the agony of his humiliation as Kerdas forced him to his knees and locked his hands in place behind his neck. Then the hated man poured the contents of one of the bowls over his crotch, and climbed back to his place.

Kneeling exposed in the centre of the table, Micah thought nothing could get much worse. Then he saw the animal. It was like a huge dog, its nose pointed, its ears hanging low like a bloodhound. Its long tongue lolled out of its mouth and it came right at Micah, leaping across the table as if it knew the treat awaiting it. Micah closed his eyes. At first it wasn't so bad, the animal's tongue working its way rhythmically over his crotch, slurping up the liquid. But when that was gone, it kept on going, working its tongue under his balls, chewing on the thong that pulled his cock backwards between his legs. It pushed its snout between the cheeks of his ass, pushing so hard that Micah fell forward, his head hitting the table. Delighted with this new angle, the creature snuffled at his asshole, its teeth beginning to nip the tender puckered flesh of his hole, stopping only to bite through the annoying thong that was in its way. The thong gave way, freeing his cock that by now was almost hard. Somehow the animal seemed to know his unwanted attentions had aroused the man and began to climb onto Micah's back, trying to fuck him with its own hairy cock. Claws ripped across his back and Micah cried out, trying to pull away, but there was no escape. It was a nightmare, the ring of flushed faces, all shouting encouragement to the animal, much as they had to the two wrestlers before, the harsh panting of the beast in his ear, the pain of the claws against his skin as he tried to crawl out from underneath the beast.

By now the creature was truly excited, growling low in its throat and humping up and down on Micah's back, its claws taking chunks out of his unprotected shoulders. Micah made one last effort to lunge out of reach of the wild beast. One of the men swung a staff at his head, knocking him unconscious. Then at last the animal came, its thin semen spurting all over the man's back and sweat-soaked hair. It climbed down, panting, saliva dripping on the comatose man who lay naked and bleeding on the platform.

Someone dragged the animal away and snapped on its leash. The excitement over, the party began breaking up, people going off in small groups, arms entwined. Dadani,

Kerdas and Attlad stood talking together for a few a
moments, before they too left, Kerdas holding the dancing-
girl's hair like a leash. No one paid the slightest attention to
the crumpled body of the unconscious slave, lying in the
centre of the table surrounded by spilled wine, broken dish-
es and half-eaten food.

FOUR

icah woke up with a pounding in his head. As he lay unmoving, it seemed as if the whole room vibrated around him. Slowly he raised himself from the slick surface of the table. He wrinkled his nose with disgust as the smells of sweat and stale wine and animal sex hit him. Cautiously he touched his aching temples and felt a trickle of blood. Checking over the rest of his body, he decided he would survive this latest attack, as he had so many others. Then the picture of Attlad, sitting at the table watching his humiliation, one hand on the lowered neck of a slave boy, flashed into his mind, making him retch. When the heaving was over, he wiped his forearm across his mouth and crawled to the edge of the table. He sat for a moment, waiting for the room to stop swaying.

The place was almost deserted, except for a few house-slaves in their brown tunics and pants, swabbing the stone floor. High on the walls, the torches still burned, casting long shadows across the silk hangings. Their indecipherable symbols looked sinister in the wavering light. He must make an effort to learn more of their language. Only this knowledge would give him the tools he needed to carry out his plan of revenge against the man who had sold him out. Right now, however, he had to get cleaned up. He looked down at the gold chain studded with pearls that hung low on his hips. It was covered with slobber from the animal's tongue.

With a growl of disgust, Micah got off the table, picked up the remains of his tunic and tied it around his waist, like a loincloth. Then he made his way to the door. The house-slaves stopped washing the floor to watch him, their faces totally impassive as the near-naked blond alien strode past.

Once he was outside in the narrow canyons he had come through hours ago in the daylight, he paused for a brief moment to look around. Above him the outlines of balconies and walkways cut into the side of the rock were visible in the bright artificial moonlight. Catwalks criss-crossed overhead, their outlines trimmed with pale blue lights. Here and there, candles flickered at windows high above him. To his right, the ground fell away abruptly and he realized there were more levels in the shadows beneath. A chill ran through him, raising goose bumps on his arms. Quickly he moved towards the light and was soon inside again. To either side stretched wide empty corridors. He had no idea where he was going, but he knew he must get clean before he would be able to make any decisions. He turned to the left, trying to retrace his steps to the courtyard and its warm spring of water gushing from the wall.

His bare feet made a soft padding noise on the stone floor. There were scarcely any landmarks along the endless corridors, only the occasional hanging ornament of twisted iron and an air grate in the ceiling. After trying a few doors that opened into even more endless rooms, he smelled the tang of fresh air and went through the double gateway that led to the courtyard.

Moonlight turned the water in the crescent-shaped pool a rippling silver. Dew lay heavy on the stone benches, glistening on the strip of carefully cropped grass around the trees. Micah pulled off his makeshift loin cloth and pissed on the ground. This simple act brought with it a sudden relaxation of muscles he hadn't even known were clenched. Defiantly he squatted down and relieved himself for the first time since his arrival, using the remains of the flimsy tunic to clean himself afterwards. Feeling more like himself, he went to the other end of the courtyard and stepped into the waterfall.

The rush of warm water stung his scraped and bruised skin painfully, but it was a cleansing feeling, natural and healing. He winced, but stood his ground under the onslaught. First he would get clean. Then he would find some clothes, go in search of Attlad, and then—

"Chento."

He spun around with a snarl of anger, crouched, ready to attack whoever it was who threatened his escape. Bar stood in the moonlight, a long sleeveless white robe covering his slender body.

Micah relaxed. "Bar."

The boy nodded. He went to a small door in the side of the wall and took out a jar and a cloth. Then he raised his arms, slid out of the robe and stepped into the warm water beside Micah.

Without another word, the boy started to rub soothing ointment on Micah's wounds, his young hands surprisingly strong as he kneaded the muscles on Micah's back and thighs. Everywhere he touched brought comfort. Micah closed his eyes, letting the magic touch unknot his muscles and his mind, until he realized the boy's fingers were talking to him.

"You are the most beautiful man I have ever seen," the signs said, dwelling sensuously on every contact between them.

It had been a long time since anyone had given Micah a compliment. Looking back on his introduction to the Citadel earlier that evening, he knew most of the men who watched him didn't desire his body for anything but ridicule. Even the women seemed disinterested, seeing not a man, but an alien slave on display for their entertainment. This boy's frank admiration stirred him. His cock twitched to life. Without thinking, he spun around and took the boy in his arms.

Startled, Bar dropped the salve.

"It's okay," Micah whispered. "I won't hurt you." He kissed the boy's shaved head, nuzzling the topknot. Finding the whip was still in place, he reached up impatiently and unscrewed the cruel attachment. Bar stiffened, obviously expecting the vicious instrument to be put to use. He didn't resist, seemed merely to prepare himself for the pain. Micah threw the whip across the courtyard where it splashed into the pool.

"I will have to swim to get it back, " Bar said, his fingers warm against Micah's cooling skin.

"Leave it there," Micah signed back.

"That is not possible. It is a part of me now, part of what I am. Being without it, would be like...amputation. I would not feel ... whole."

"Who's whipping boy are you, Bar?"

"I belong to the lady Dadani, just as you do. I am one of her sex-toys, but Kerdas is the real master here."

"Kerdas," muttered Micah.

"Sshhh." The boy led Micah out of the water and produced towels for them which he proceeded to use first on Micah, then himself. Micah took the towels and laid them on the soft grass under one of the trees. He took Bar's hand and drew him down beside him, looking into the great dark eyes as they filled with longing. Here was a young man who had never felt another man's hand deal anything but pain, who had grown to accept that as natural, but who longed for something else, something he probably had no name for.

Micah looked at the pale body, marble white in the moonlight except where angry scars showed where the whip had broken the skin. The knob of his mutilated cock pushed up between his legs, free for once of the mockery of the blue and silver beads. Micah touched the shiny pink skin, stretched taut over the small mushroom of the head, and heard Bar catch his breath.

"Easy," Micah murmured, sliding his fingers along the short shaft to the balls, smooth as glass, and just as hard. They were like steel spheres to his touch. The boy was panting now, catching his breath, panting again. He looked a little frightened. Micah slid his whole hand underneath the hard balls, up the crack of his ass to the tight little asshole.

He paused. "Just relax," he whispered, knowing the boy would infer the meaning from the tone. Bar turned his head and fastened his mouth on Micah's right tit, sucking strongly as Micah slid a finger into his ass. To his surprise, the hole was not as tight as he expected. They had probably stuffed the boy with a great many large objects of one sort or another, he thought, sliding a few more fingers into the warm velvet dampness. Bar began to whimper, little moans of pleasure as he pressed closer to Micah, sucking his nipples as if his life depended on swallowing the pumped up tits. He began to rub his loins on Micah's muscular thigh, faster and faster, until with a strangled cry, smothered on Micah's chest, his little cock shot a load of come. The boy burst into tears.

"Don't cry," murmured Micah, glancing over his shoulder nervously at the open door. It was getting lighter in the small patch of sky above them. Would someone come along here soon? Another slave? One of the women? Bar suddenly scrambled out of his grasp and buried his face between Micah's legs. Hot tears ran over the tender shaved skin of Micah's crotch as Bar's experienced tongue lapped under that heavy cock, exploring the underside down to his balls, licking the stiffening shaft as he uttered soft moans of delight. He opened his mouth and took the tip between his lips, sucking gently, gently, as he slowly took in more and more of the alien man's quivering cock. Micah suppressed a moan of pleasure, reaching out to caress the delicate skull, so frail under the boy's shaved head. Micah's world centred now on the boy's warm mouth sealed around him. His felt his balls tighten and closed his eyes as the first hot waves of pleasure rolled over him. His fingers closed convulsively on the boy's head and still that eager mouth gulped and strained to swallow his spurting come. The boy's throat muscles worked overtime until at last Micah's cock was milked dry.

Micah rolled over on his back, a wonderful languor seeping through his body. Even as he enjoyed the experience, his mind was busy with his plans for a future free of this place, and the memory of Attlad's treachery unavenged.

A gentle splash in the pool told him Bar was retrieving the whip. Propping his head on his hand, he watched the boy dry himself off, then clip the long leather tresses to his own dark topknot of hair.

Bar gazed down at him, his eyes serious. "You must sleep now." His fingers moved swiftly in the air. "Come with me. I'll take you to our place." The boy slipped on his long tunic and started across the courtyard. He paused at a small door in the wall and was surprised to find Micah right behind him.

Micah smiled grimly. It seemed he hadn't forgotten his old training as a Nebula Warrior. That, at least, was comforting. As he followed his guide through the labyrinth of dim passages, he concentrated on making a mental map of the twists and turns, plotting it in his mind as if it were one of the many star charts he had carried in his head so easily in his days as a navigator. These hallways were quite different from the public corridors he had been in before. Colour was everywhere, becoming more intense the further they went, until his eyes were dazzled by the brilliant radiance of it, even in the soft lighting. There were no flaring torches here, but what looked like candlelight, glowing from banks of candelabra against the walls.

Bar pushed his way through arched double doors and Micah followed him into a round antechamber. He blinked in the sudden light. A big man dressed in a short tunic and loose pants reclining on a bench at the side of the room, motioned to Bar to approach him. Even from the back, Micah saw the boy blush as he obeyed and held up his long robe above his waist. The man picked up what looked like a cage of silver wire and blue beads and fitted the contraption over the boy's little cock and between his balls. Micah stepped closer to watch as the man fastened it with a hand held instrument that reminded Micah of a tiny riveter. The boy jerked as a loud click sounded. The man laughed.

"You're lucky I let you take it off at all," he said, and slapped the boy's thigh. "Such pretty little jewels should be shown off all the time. Now get in there and take him with you. And remember, the switch is set to on." He gave the cock in its jewelled cage a final tweak and lay down again. He barely glanced at Micah before closing his eyes.

Micah studied him for a moment. The man was big, but soft. He would be an easy victory if it came to a fight. Satisfied, Micah followed Bar into the dim room beyond.

Behind him, the heavy door swung shut. A lock clicked into place.

Before him was a series of rooms, all opening into each other. A hallway led through the middle, curving as if the whole place were in a tower of some sort, or maybe it was just because these people liked curves in their architecture. Slim pillars clustered every ten feet or so, but they seemed to have little purpose except to be decorative and divide the space into small circular areas. Every inch of the walls and even the domed ceilings were covered with bright colour, overlaid with silver designs and symbols similar to what was on the silken hangings. Half naked boys lay about, sleeping on cushions in the small areas. Their heads were shaved like Bar's and they all wore the gold and pearl girdles low on their hips.

"It's like a harem," Micah whispered to himself, and the idea both fascinated and appalled him. Why was the sexual activity at the camp acceptable, even desirable, and yet this setup made his stomach churn? The problem was easily answered. This system brought his manhood into question, something that had never happened before. He grimaced as he followed Bar into one of the round areas. To his surprise, he found the space was surrounded on three sides by a curved plastic wall. Once they were inside, an almost invisible door slid to, shutting them in with a distinct click.

Micah swung around and tried to pry the door open with his strong hands, but his sweaty palms slid helplessly over the smooth surface. There was nothing to get a grip on.

"Fucking hell!" he exploded, pounding his fist on the clear wall. His voice was unexpectedly loud in the small space. He swung around to find Bar watching him with frightened eyes. Micah shrugged apologetically and threw himself on the cushions piled luxuriantly on the platform that filled about half the little room. Outside their capsule, the others lay about, each enclosed in his own invisible cage, on display for whoever walked through. Now he understood why there had been no noise as he walked by, no sighs or sounds of breathing, no rustle of silk as one of the boys turned over in his sleep, showing his pale ass.

"Who are all these boys?" he signed to Bar.

"We belong to the lady Dadani," he replied, kneeling down beside Micah. "She uses us when she wishes, or hands us to her friends. Whatever she wants, or Kerdas asks for," he added.

"If you're always locked in, how is it you were allowed out tonight?"

The boy dropped his eyes. "That guard at the door, he likes me. He lets me out sometimes, if I do favours for him, and tonight I wanted to find you before Kerdas sent someone."

"Thanks."

Micah looked more closely at the boy in the cubicle next to them. He lay on his back and Micah could see that he, too, had a jewelled cage contraption over his stubby cock. He turned back to Bar and touched the silver that surrounded his penis. The wire was surprisingly strong.

"It's our night keeper," Bar explained. "If we're asleep, a signal from it will wake us. And this way we cannot pleasure ourselves, or another," he added sadly, gazing at Micah's large flaccid cock. "Pleasure is only for the masters."

"So you don't even have the dignity of self discipline," Micah murmured to himself. It made sense, in a way. Bar had probably not chosen to be a slave, as he had.

Bar looked at him questioningly.

"How did you become a slave?" Micah asked.

"It was decided when I was born. I always knew I would be a sex slave, for a time, at least, until I am too old. If I make it that far, I go to the temple. Then it will be a good life. Like the others, I went through the ceremony at ten. Then I did the training for five years, and I was chosen by my lady to be one of her boys. I have been serving here for four years."

"The ceremony?"

Bar blushed and dropped his eyes. "We are taught the arts of sex by the priests and priestesses, shown what our masters and mistresses might want from us. We are made sterile to keep us youthful and smooth. We have the docking done so our cocks will be thick and short, to look good and give more pleasure to our lady. Besides, only the husbands or lovers should reach that most intimate space inside, no?" He looked at Micah anxiously, as if afraid this alien male might not understand the subtleties of his culture.

"Shit," muttered Micah. "They have mutilated you for their own pleasure," he signed.

"It is their right," Bar replied simply.

Micah shook his head, but realized it would do no good to argue the point with the boy. He had known little about the Kudites before the crash that brought him here, but his people had known about the existence of slaves. There had been plenty of rumours about sex slaves, too, but no one had guessed how complex the system was.

"What do you do the rest of the time?" Micah asked.

"We are all expected to work at some decorative craft, depending on our talents and what we were taught in the temple. Some of the boys are expert design artists and spend long hours during the day working on the robes and cloaks worn by our lady and her sisters. That boy over there works with jewels. Some of the designs on the walls are done by the boys."

"And you?"

"I paint miniatures." He dropped his eyes shyly. It was

clear he was not used to talking about himself. His slender hands fluttered uncertainly in his lap.

Micah had to touch his knee to get him to watch the signs again. "Will you speak out loud as you sign to me? I want to learn your language better."

"To hear my voice saying the words I sign will not help. I do not speak the way the masters speak. Many of the words are the same, but the sound is very different. Where I grew up, I was taught the language of slaves only. Is that what you want to learn?"

A beam of bright light caught Micah's attention and he swung his head around to see Kerdas strolling among the islands of half-naked boys, his sleeping robe knotted carelessly about his waist. His face was flushed with wine and he was smiling, as if at some secret joke. The light came from a small torch, the flames leaping up so even and white it looked unnatural. Beside him, Micah felt Bar tense and then hastily pull off his robe. The marks of Kerdas's whip still flamed on his pale skin. As Micah watched, Bar lay back on the cushions, hands above his head, legs apart, showing his caged, shaved crotch to the visitor. His dark eyes were suddenly glazed and vacant.

The visitor had stopped right next to their cubicle, where the boy with the small brand on his ass still slept, blissfully unaware of his audience. Micah watched Kerdas, that face so much like Attlad's, yet so different. Kerdas didn't look directly at him, but he got the clear cold feeling that what was about to happen was for his benefit as much as the for the Kudite's pleasure.

Without warning, the boy catapulted from the bed, his mouth stretched wide in a scream, his hands clawing the air around his wired crotch, obviously unable to gain any relief. Kerdas strode inside the enclosure and grabbed the boy's hands. He pulled them above his head, and attached them to the pillar at one side of the sleeping platform. On closer inspection, Micah saw that the twining vine-like decorations disguised clamps and manacles that now held the boy helpless by his slender wrists. His whole body jerked spasmodically, his little knob of a cock twitching behind its jewels, the slit gleaming with pre-come.

Kerdas raised the torch and touched one of the boy's tits with the flame. As the boy's mouth stretched impossibly wider, Kerdas pulled something out of his pocket and thrust what looked like a large ball into the boy's mouth. He attached it there firmly by tying the leather thongs hanging from each side around the back of the boy's head. By this time, the kid's face was beet red, his dark eyes wide with pain, panic, shock. His narrow chest heaved spasmodically.

Micah found his own cock reacting to the scene, in spite of his intellectual revulsion to the mindless cruelty. Kerdas's carelessly worn robe was open to the waist, revealing thick swirls of black body hair on the man's broad chest. Sweat broke out on Micah's forehead as his eyes moved back to the boy, drawn to the scene almost against his will.

Saliva drooled from the stretched corners of the boy's mouth, dripped shiny on his chin, emphasizing his utter helplessness. It was soon evident that Kerdas was controlling an electric charge of some sort that connected with the wire cock-cage, by squeezing a small box in the palm of his hand. The boy's back jerked in an arch against the pain as shock after shock jolted through him. Kerdas put the torch in a sconce on the wall and stripped off his robe with one hand, the other still pressing the box.

Kerdas's big cock was only half hard. His mouth set in a line, he flung the cushions and silken covers from the sleeping platform and activated a button under one edge. A shelf sprung into view and at the sight of it, the boy's eyes nearly rolled up into his head in fear. Dropping the box onto the bed, Kerdas reached up and unhooked the boy. In one brutal motion, he flung the pliant naked body across the sturdy bar projecting at right angles from the bed and attached his manacles to a ring in the floor. After a moment's thought, he slipped a short length of chain around the boy's right ankle and attached it to another ring. Kicking the legs wide apart, he did the same to the other ankle. Everything he did, Micah noticed, was done quickly, with practised ease, as if he were interested only in the outcome of the procedure. So different from the passionate involvement of Attlad .... Micah blinked.

When he looked again, Kerdas was sticking small silver disks on the boy's ass, one on each cheek. He grabbed a fistful of the long braided topknot and clipped the end onto the chain of pearls he wore around his waist, in such a way that his head was pulled back at an awkward angle, and his red face was clearly visible, its mouth stretched grotesquely with the wooden ball, saliva drooling over his chin. The dark eyes were filled with pain and the humiliating knowledge that this man's brutality was providing something that he had learned to crave.

Micah heard a whimper from Bar behind him, but he didn't turn his head. He was rivetted to the strange silent scene of agony. Kerdas held the box, his thumb pushing the button on the side and smiling with sadistic pleasure as the boy's ass cheeks began to dance as the electric current jumped through the rosy skin. It was odd, Micah thought dispassionately, how that pale ass was now reddening as if a hand had warmed the trembling flesh. He found himself getting hot at the thought of how that skin would feel under his own hand; how it would quiver and vibrate slightly, as the force of the blow shook the cheek, leaving the imprint of his hand. He felt his nuts tighten, his heart begin to race, and he knew this whole show was for his benefit, to make him acknowledge the power of cruelty to arouse even the reluctant alien slave.

The boy's eyes had rolled up into his head, and his slender neck was trembling with the strain of being pulled back at that unnatural angle. Kerdas had apparently set the charge button on the box and put it down, while he leaned against the bed, legs spread wide, and masturbated. His strokes were hard and rough, his thick cock barely contained by his fist. Suddenly he jumped up and forced his engorged cock into the boy's ass in one swift terrible thrust. The boy's body went rigid, then his head flopped to the side in a faint. His flesh continued to jump and jerk as the power surged through him and now through Kerdas cock as well, as the man pounded in and out of the inert form, fucking the sex slave, his face a mask of lust. His mouth opened in a silent roar as he came, pumping his seed into the unconscious boy. After a moment, he pulled out, wiped off his dick on the boy's back and pulled on his robe. As he tied the sash, he looked right at Micah and smiled. There was triumph and hatred and sated lust. And Micah suddenly realized that his own cock was rigid, standing straight out, reaching towards the man behind the glass. Micah set his jaw, refusing to drop his eyes as he resisted the temptation to cover himself with the silken bed coverings.

Beside him, Bar suddenly cried out. Micah turned and saw the boy, his hands clenched, his cock jerking.

"Stop!" shouted Micah and whirled around to face the boy's tormentor.

But Kerdas only laughed at him. Then he raised his hands and signed: "Soon you, too, will be able to feel the surge of pain. You'll get off on that, boy, and so will I! Soon. In a short time you will stand with the other pearlboys at the bonding ceremony of your former master, no longer a man, but an exotic toy for others." With that, he took down the torch, turned on his heel and strode out of the room.

Micah swore and knelt beside his companion. "Are you all right?" he signed.

"It is nothing," Bar assured him, blushing. "He didn't really want to hurt me. It's you he wants."

"Why? And what did he mean with that last remark? Did you see it?"

"I saw, yes. He spoke about your docking, and about the bonding ceremony—the marriage of our lady and your old master, Attlad. You understand?"

Micah felt a cold shock hit him in the belly like a blow.

"It's almost a pity," Bar went on and looked down at Micah's waning erection. The red dragon of Attlad was still clear along the shaft. "It will cut the dragon in half."

FIVE

ours passed, and still Micah's mind raced with images of a double betrayal. Attlad, tossing him aside was a bitter enough pill to swallow. Coldly handing him over as a gift to his bride, however, was even worse. Was he meant as a token of what Attlad was giving up for her? Or, more likely, had Micah meant nothing more than a toy he was now passing on, a plaything that was no longer needed. He knew that some men made love with other men only because there were no women available. Was this the custom with the Kudite warriors?

Bar slept peacefully, curled against his chest, but Micah could take no comfort from the warm trusting presence. Across the boy's shaved head, the Terran's steel blue eyes stared into the neighbouring cubicle, barely aware of the dark-clad house- slaves who finally came to unshackle the still unconscious form of the beaten boy and carry him away.

The coldness inside had not abated when a series of chimes sounded the wake-up call and the invisible doors slid open. Micah followed Bar's lead, walking naked through the chamber, now filled with drowsy boys, rubbing their eyes as they filed out of their cubicles. Once in the line, they were strangely quiet, eyes downcast, hands clasped behind their backs, bare feet shuffling silently over the brightly coloured tiles. They passed an ornate spiral staircase that twisted out of sight high above them, then went through a door into an echoing grey room. Just inside the doorway, stood a man in the scarlet tunic and baggy pants which seemed to be a sort of uniform. Each boy paused in front of him, legs apart, hips thrust forward, while the man grasped the jewelled cage and unclipped it, releasing the misshapen shaved genitals. He gave Micah's large cock a dark look, then waved him on into the echoing room.

A gallery ran around it above their heads. Several men and women lounged over the railing, watching the parade below, chatting with each other. Visitors or friends of the family, Micah thought to himself wryly, and then he spotted Dadani among them. It occurred to him that she may have brought them to see him, since they were all obviously interested in the tall blond alien male, pointing him out to each other and laughing and chatting with animation. He looked away and squared his shoulders. They would get no extra amusement at his expense!

The dozen or so boys lined up in the middle of the room, Micah beside Bar near the middle. Without warning, countless jets of icy water hit them from all sides. Micah bit his lip to keep from crying out, as some of them did, even though they must have known what to expect. Just as he was getting used to the icy temperature, the water grew suddenly hotter, until it was all he could do to keep from trying to get away from the scalding spray. Around him, he saw the pale skin of the boys turn lobster red. Several of them appeared to be sobbing, and when the water suddenly stopped, their cries echoed strangely, mixed with the casual chatter of the onlookers. Beside him, Bar whimpered, trying to catch his breath.

One of the handlers clapped his hands and the boy at the end of the line stepped forward, spun around, spread his legs wide and bent over. It was all done as one smooth movement, his hands sliding down to part his ass cheeks so the handler could inspect his asshole. Casually, the man shoved a silver spigot about three inches long up the boy's hole, held it a few moments and pulled it out, releasing a stream of water. He slapped the boy's ass and he stood up at once, walking to the far side of the room to the feeding station, as water leaked out of his hole and dribbled down his legs.

Just before it was his turn, Micah spotted the dark-skinned eunuch wrestler he had lost the match to on the ship. He was off by himself, leaning one elbow on the railing while he chewed thoughtfully on something in held in his hand. Stunned, Micah missed his cue to step forward and had to suffer the ignominy of being slapped to get his attention. Gritting his teeth, he forced himself to imitate what the others had done. He bent over and opened himself for the invasion of the water. Nothing happened. He tensed. A finger slipped inside, rubbing his joy spot slowly, sensuously. This was far worse than what he had been expecting. It was something he was helpless to fight or ignore. His body yearned to respond, his hole hungry to be filled. A small moan escaped him, unnoticed. The man's other hand began to hit Micah's ass, in time with the hidden strokes of his finger — slap — stroke — slap — stroke — His cock, already half hard, began to lengthen, as his sphincter muscle sucked greedily at the fleshy finger that fucked him. It seemed like a long time since he had been fucked even this much. The backs of his legs began to tremble. He felt the quivers passing through the muscles, communicating the erotic charge to his hands, his wrists, his arms. His shoulder muscles jumped. His face flushed wine red as pre-come drooled from his slit. He could barely analyse the hollow noise echoing around him, and then he realized it was laughter and his flush deepened with his shame. He had forgotten his audience, these people who rarely had a real man to tease and torment, a man with a big cock and a set of real balls to slap and humiliate. But the excruciating ordeal was over abruptly as the silver spigot was thrust up his ass, the sudden pain almost welcome. A sharp backhanded slap on his ass signalled the end of the cleansing. He straightened up. Dizzy, his cock still hard and unsatisfied, he walked unsteadily to the next stop, the feeding platform near the door. He went up the three steps to where a row of silver bottles was fastened to the waist high railing.

"Kneel."

He did so, legs apart, hands behind his back, as the others had done. He braced himself for the next ordeal, but his stomach was complaining loudly of hunger. There was nothing to be gained by refusing to eat. The handler grinned as he pulled a rubber teat from his pocket and fitted it to the silver bottle on the stand. It was large, much bigger than the nipples on the other bottles. With a hot rush of embarrassment, Micah realized it reassembled a good sized cock. Before he could react, the handler grabbed his damp hair and pulled his head forward, forcing the teat of the silver bottle into his mouth. Micah closed his eyes and tried not to think of that muscular black/green wrestler watching his humiliation, or the women and their guests, amused to see a Nebula Warrior on his knees, sucking at a rubber teat shaped like a cock. He had to admit that it felt good in his mouth. He sucked greedily, thankful for the thick milky liquid that oozed down his throat, even though he recognized the slight bitter taste of the tranquillizer drug he had been fed before, back at the Complex. He wished it were strong enough to blot out his surroundings, but he knew from experience this wouldn't happen.

His eyes snapped open as he felt the man's hands on his cock. At once he tensed.

"Keep sucking," the man ordered.

Micah obeyed, his cheeks going hollow as he pulled strongly at the thick milk while the handler snapped a rubber keeper just under the head of his cock and pulled it back though his legs by the attached thong. Micah winced as he felt his cock bent backwards, then gasped as ice touched his balls, making them retract suddenly. The man's fingers pushed his nuts skilfully up inside his body. The narrow strip of leather cut against his asshole as it was clipped to the pearl belt he wore, thus keeping his balls in their uncomfortable hiding place.

The handler pulled him away from the teat. He was laughing. As a parting insult, he rubbed scented oil onto the naked crotch and presented his fingers to be licked. Staring straight ahead, Micah sucked the man's fingers clean.

"Now go. Get dressed. And do not try to touch your genitals. If you have to piss, you must ask permission. Understand?"

Micah nodded, his face red. He got to his feet and made his way to the door where the other boys had gone. He found himself in a room lined on one side with shelves full of colourful filmy clothing and on the other, a series of cubicles, each with its own cupboard supplied with all manner of bottles and creams and cosmetics. Here the boys were dried off, their skin rubbed with delicately scented oils. Some of them had rosy colour rubbed into their little nipples. Some put on make-up to accentuate the size of their eyes. And they all had their heads shaved every day.

"It depends on what the mistress or the guests ask for," one of the handlers explained curtly. "You'll have to have your body hair removed each day, until the operation makes all that work unnecessary. Stand on this platform." He unclipped Micah's cock and proceeded to spray green gel over his body. Then starting with his face and ending with his ass-crack, he scraped it off, removing all traces of hair. This done, he rubbed a pink cream over the reddened skin and performed the same ritual with his poor cock as the man with the bottles had done. "Awful lot of work," he grumbled. "Here. You dress him."

Micah was passed along to the next man, who pulled a fine-spun mauve tunic over the Terran's head and arranged it so the gold nipple rings and the chain between them were in plain view. The tunic was short, and open to the waist. A belt of deep purple and seed pearls held it in place, but the garment made Micah feel more vulnerable than when he had been naked. When he moved, his cock pulled painfully between his legs, and the fine silk whispered against his shaven sexless crotch. The perfume wafting from his own skin set his teeth on edge.

Micah learned that this morning routine never varied. Everything seemed almost choreographed, as if done to a rigid system. His military training took a strange sort of comfort from the pattern. Any order was better than the chaos his life had suddenly become. From now on, he was not allowed to leave the Quarters, as the pearlboys' area was called. He was always barefoot, always nearly naked. The tunic was so short his cock would have been plainly visible, if it hadn't been pulled up out of sight. He learned to go a long time without pissing.

Although the other boys appeared to have their assigned tasks, Micah was seen as a plaything, a novelty for his mistress, her guests and even his fellow slaves. That first

day was a holiday of some sort for the Kudites, but for
Micah, it set a humiliating pattern. In the morning, he was
taken to where Dadani and a group of her friends were
painting, some on large blocks of grey paper, others deco-
rating bits of cut out metal. Micah was told to stand on a
platform and pose, holding one of the metal ornaments. All
morning he stood there, trying to hold the various poses he
was ordered to assume. Finally, one of the women came and
tucked up his tunic, then pushed down on his neck so he
was bent over, exposing his ass. After a few moments of dis-
cussion with the other women, she pulled the tunic off completely, and arranged his long hair so it trailed on the floor
artistically at his feet.

It seemed like hours he hung there, holding his ankles,
his face red from the awkward position, his muscles screaming for release, while the women sketched and chattered
and laughed. When they tired of painting on paper, his
ordeal was not over. They gathered around their living stat-
ue and began to paint his skin. At first they were hesitant,
giggling as they drew a brush in circles on his shoulders, first
one side, then the other to match it. One of them dipped
her delicate brush on the tip of his cock where it peeked up
between the crack in his ass. He jerked and shivered from
the contact, bringing gales of laughter from them. Someone
unclipped the leather thong from its pearl clasp and his
cock sprang free. As they watched, fascinated, his nuts slowly reappeared.

"Come with me," Dadani commanded, and he was surprised he recognized the words before seeing the signs.
Using the thong attached to his cock as a leash, she led him
from the room and through the corridor, out past the
entrance to the Quarters. When he balked at going naked
outside the private area, she merely tugged hard at his cock
and he followed.

It wasn't far, but the public hall was crowded at this hour and everyone paused to look at the blond alien male, whose member was so shamefully stiff and long, following his mistress like a dog. Micah, who had always been so proud of his body, for the first time wished he were less well developed so he would blend more easily with the slender boys and women who surrounded him.

Dadani led him to a small bright room, hung with beautiful tapestries, the first he had seen depicting naked men and women. Several guests were already seated at the low tables, piled high with food, among them, Kerdas. Dadani motioned Micah up on the table between her seat and Kerdas. Obediently he stepped up among the piles of fruit and steaming bowls of coloured spicy rice, his mouth watering at the smells. His throat was dry, too, since nothing had passed his lips since the thick milky breakfast he had sucked from the silver bottle early that morning. Following the signals from his owner, he squatted down among the plates and platters, one more colourful delicacy for the guests' enjoyment. Something warm and soft squashed against his balls.

"Our alien friend does not look happy," Kerdas remarked, tweaking the thong that now lay on the table. "You ladies are not treating him well. Are you thirsty, boy?"

Although his throat was parched, Micah didn't reply, not trusting the man or his interest.

"Here, hold this goblet of wine," Kerdas went on. "You might be thirsty later. High. Higher, above your head. Now, don't spill one drop, or you will be punished. Understand?"

Micah nodded, careful to keep the heavy gold goblet steady between his hands.

"Good. Maybe you will be allowed to have a drink later if you obey."

"Perhaps he is hungry," suggested another man, entering into the spirit of the game. "I can do something about that."

At a careless nod from Dadani, the man got to his feet and walked around behind Micah. Next thing, he felt something shoved hard up his asshole. He flinched, his muscles contracting, trying to expel the object, while all the time he was aware that the goblet above his head was reacting to his spasm.

"Relax and it will go easier," Kerdas signed, grinning.

Micah felt his asshole stuffed, something hard and long being forced up inside him. Whatever it was, stretched him cruelly, steadily. Tears sprang to his eyes as he began to tremble. There had to be a good five inches up inside him now, and still the man kept shoving.

"Vegetables," Kerdas signed. "Good for a growing warrior." He laughed. "Now some fruit, Perin. Our friend must have a well rounded diet."

Micah's tormentor choose a small pear from the table and handed it to the man behind him. Once again Micah felt his asshole forced wide, and now his arms began to shake uncontrollably, splashing red wine on his naked shoulders and chest, where it blended with the paint.

"You'll pay for that," Kerdas signed. He took a metal ball from the display in the middle of another table and attached it to the chain suspended from Micah's nipple rings. The ball was heavy, and as Kerdas dropped it, the weight pulled unmercifully on Micah's tits. His arms trembled even more, spilling more of the wine on his blond hair.

"You have no discipline," Kerdas remarked. "This does not surprise me. My brother, too, is quite the undisciplined savage." He said a few things to Dadani, who laughed and sent one of the boys out of the room, obviously to fetch something. "You will learn, boy."

Micah tried to control the shaking in his limbs, his thighs, from the squatting position he was forced to maintain, his arms from being held up so long. With concentration, he managed to keep utterly still, with only the occasional shudder to give him away. Ahead of him, he noticed a pearlboy he didn't recognize. The boy was very pretty, naked except for the jewels displaying his tiny cock and a silver collar around his neck. At a signal, he knelt beside one of the women who offered him her distended right breast. Eagerly, he leaned against her, opening his mouth to her nipple. She continued to talk and eat while he suckled, obviously feeding. Fascinated, Micah watched the quick sucking motion of his soft cheeks, the dreamy heavy-lidded eyes. The boy's tiny cock glistened with pre-come. After a while, she pushed him gently away for a moment and then held out her left breast to him. Again he sucked greedily, his hands clasped behind his back.

Micah was so engrossed in the scene, he didn't notice the return of the servant, who held out a tray with small brass bells on it to Kerdas.

"Now comes the test," he signed. He bound two of the bells to Micah's cock with silk, then reached up and tweaked his left nipple. Already sore from the weights, there was still a quick response from the Terran, whose tits had been made very sensitive by Attlad's constant attention. Kerdas smiled. He got to his feet and walked around behind Micah, who still squatted on the table, holding the goblet above his head, his muscles shining with sweat at his exertions. Slowly, with exquisite cruelty, Kerdas pushed his thumb up into the already stuffed asshole, massaging Micah's prostate.

The Terran's cock began to rise from the table, swelling, growing, the tattooed dragon now plainly visible. Micah felt the tears spill out of this eyes as his big cock began to jerk uncontrollably, ringing the bells. The guests all clapped and laughed and drank a toast to Kerdas, who had thought up this great holiday entertainment. With a smothered cry,

Micah felt his balls churning and knew he couldn't hold back much longer. Just as he thought he couldn't stand it, Kerdas thrust two fingers inside him and Micah began to whimper. He couldn't come! The thong was still tight around his cock, preventing any release. His cock jerked and spasmed, ringing the bells merrily as Micah shook, and trembled, spilling red wine on his shoulders and back and heaving chest.

"Don't you dare come," Kerdas signed on his skin, his fingers biting viciously into the ass muscle. "Don't you dare."

"I can't... Please... Please, Kerdas!" Micah flung back his head in a passionate plea to his tormentor, not caring that the words themselves meant nothing to the man. The intent was unmistakable. Hearing his own pleading voice was one more humiliation.

Kerdas low cruel laughter thrummed in his ear. With a final jab, his fingers were gone from Micah's ass, which was still stretched wide, stuffed with offerings from the table beneath him. Kerdas walked around and thrust his fingers in Micah's mouth to be cleaned. The slave obeyed.

Micah spent the rest of the time, while they finished their meal, squatting there, on display, his unsatisfied cock so stiff it held the brass bells off the table, still grasping the now almost empty goblet above his head. His sphincter muscles strained to contain the mess of food deep inside him, his thighs thrummed with the tension caused by the long held pose. Sweat poured from his naked body, smudging the paint, mingling with the spilt wine. For the most part, Dadani and her guests seemed to have tired of him, and they continued their conversation, barely even glancing in his direction.

Except for Kerdas. Micah could feel his cold animosity, even though the man barely seemed aware of him now. He knew there would be more to endure from this man. And he was right.

When the others left, Kerdas lingered behind, paying no attention to the house-slaves and servers who began to clear up the feast around him. He knocked the golden goblet from Micah's numb grasp and pulled him off the table by his sweat-soaked hair.

"You are hungry?"

Micah shook his head.

"Don't lie to me, slave!" Kerdas hit him across the face, the force of the blow almost knocking him off balance. "I can hear your belly growling for food. Are you hungry?"

This time Micah nodded. It was true. He was ravenous, his hunger fuelled by having spent the last two hours watching others eat, smelling the delicious aromas of spices and meat and sugared fruit. His throat ached for food and drink. He would have drooled, had his throat not been so parched.

Kerdas nodded with satisfaction. "Then you will eat. Get up on the table in front of me."

Micah moved stiffly to obey, but it was difficult to climb up, without releasing what was inside him. At last he pushed his ass cheeks together with his hands while he crawled awkwardly up on the marble platform in front of Kerdas.

"Squat and release what's in your ass."

With a sigh of relief, Micah let go. The mass crammed up almost to his bowels rushed out with a sickening splat, accompanied by a loud fart. Micah flushed as the acrid smell rose around him.

Kerdas's lips curled into a sneer. "Get down on all fours, animal, and eat. Now!"

Micah, his face red, bent over the hodge-podge of rice and pieces of cucumber and long squash, flavoured with his own shit. For a moment, bile rose in his mouth, but he swallowed it and began to eat, making his mind a blank. When it was all gone, he raised his head.

"Now for your drink," Kerdas said. He stood in front of the crouching Micah, pulled out his cock and thrust it into the other man's mouth. Before Micah could react, a stream of hot piss hit the back of his throat, almost gagging him, but Kerdas held the end of the thong attached to his cock and he pulled viciously at the first sign of rebellion. Micah swallowed.

When it was over, Kerdas smiled with satisfaction. Micah's cock was still stiff, unsatisfied. He knew he would get nothing from Kerdas. The Kudite yanked the thong back between his legs and clipped it in place.

"Maybe next time you'll follow orders better. If you do, you might get a reward."

With that cryptic sign, he turned and left Micah crouching naked on the table, his throbbing cock fastened between his legs.

This kind of random teasing torture became a feature of his days. He was wretched. Here he was a slave without a master, a man taught to long for another's cock to plug him, another's rough hand to train him. He needed someone to serve! Although he was owned by Dadani, he did not 'belong' to her, as he had to Attlad. She did not want him to satisfy her. There was no desire in what she did to him. He was a plaything, enjoyed by Kerdas more than anyone else. And Micah knew that for Kerdas, every indignity suffered by Micah, was meant for Attlad. That, too, was hard to bear.

One morning, after the public cleansing and feeding was over, he was told someone wanted to see him. Following one of the house-slaves, he was ushered to a part of the

Quarters he hadn't been in before.

He found himself in a small intimate room with a deep window seat piled with cushions. Outside the 'window' was a painted scene of sunshine and green grass, and lounging there in the artificial sunlight, was the huge black wrestler, one muscular leg bent under him. He, too, wore a tunic, but his was longer than Micah's, and he wore leggings underneath. He lay back and studied the Terran insolently, one hand fingering the ivory amulet that hung from a leather thong around his neck.

"You!" Micah hissed though clenched teeth. He had often noticed the man watching in the public gallery as the boys were washed and fed. Micah hated him. The man was the physical embodiment of his betrayal. If only he hadn't lost the match, maybe—

"Charmed, I'm sure," said the man.

Micah was so stunned to hear the English words, especially with a slight but unmistakable British accent, that he merely stared.

"The Nebula Warrior has lost his voice along with his balls?" the deep voice went on, taunting.

"Who are you and what so you want?" growled Micah, giving his adversary the cool glare that used to so disconcert his men back at the base.

This man merely stared back and rolled his heavy shoulders as if limbering his muscles for action. "You want a program? Okay, here's the line up: I am Grir-rad-Dalet, you are Chento-rad-Dadani."

"That is not who I am," Micah replied, his eyes narrowing as he looked at Grir. "I doubt that it says much about who you are, either."

"You got that right." The man laughed, a rich harsh masculine sound that was music to Micah's ears in this smothering place. "Let me put it this way: You were

Chento-rad-Attlad. I was Grir-rad-Montgomery."

Micah flushed. "Stop playing games! What the hell—"
He stopped, his brain suddenly registering the last part of
Grir's remark. "Montgomery. Reed Montgomery? The probe
pilot?"

"Good. You were listening."

"Let me get this straight. You're saying you 'belonged' to
Reed Montgomery, from Earth Base Gamma 1?" The man
nodded. "But that's impossible! Terran's don't 'own' people.
Besides, he was here 10 years ago with the initial contact
team."

Again the man nodded. "There was no official base
then, no strict rules and regulations saying what we could or
could not do. We lived in a makeshift cabin on the edge of
the red desert. He taught me English," he added, with evident pride. "The Kudites don't know how well I speak it. For
a long time after he left, it was a private thing for me. I
think you can understand what I mean."

It was Micah's turn to nod. For a brief moment the
inscrutable face had let him glimpse a deep personal lose,
and in that moment, he knew that Grir loved his Terran
pilot fiercely, that his was a story every bit as striking and
unusual as Micah's own. He, too, appeared to have given up
a lot for love. But that story would have to wait.

"Okay, so that explains a little," he said carefully, still
not ready to trust this man who had been the instrument of
his downfall. "But what do you want from me?"

"What every slave of my position wants: more status."

Micah snorted derisively. "Status? A slave?"

"You have no understanding of how things work here,
Chento. Have you not wondered why I am dressed and you
are nearly naked? Why I wander around at will, while you
cannot leave the women's area without permission? You are
not a Personal Bodyslave to a warrior any longer, Chento.

Now, you are nothing. Your mistress has no desire for such as you. Surely you realize that by now?"

"Then why am I here? Why was I sent here?"

"You lost the game," he said. His face was serious, searching Micah's for a few moments after he spoke.

"It was more than that, wasn't it?" Micah said softly.

The man didn't answer. He looked away from Micah for a moment, his bald head gleaming like polished green-flecked ebony in the sunlight. "I am not satisfied with the outcome of our match," he said at last.

"*You're* not satisfied!" exclaimed Micah. "You think I am? God damn it, man! I lost everything!"

Grir waited till his outburst died away. "I want to win a fight with a Nebula Warrior who is not drunk, who has all his faculties. Otherwise it means nothing."

"Shit!" muttered Micah. "Any time you want a rematch, just name it. I'll be there."

Grir smiled, the same haughty supercilious look that had enraged Micah before. "You forget. You have no say in it, Chento."

"My name is Micah Starion."

"You are Chento, and you are a slave."

"What game are you playing here, Grir?" said Micah, softly.

"We are both on the same team, mate." For once the language sounded strained and unnatural. "Look at it this way. If we have a rematch, you will have to train. This will keep you occupied, put off the inevitable 'docking' operation that will take away your manhood, and get you away from all this perfume and silk. This is to your advantage, no?"

"That's true. What's the advantage to you?"

"Status, as I said. I'm a professional fighter and I'm ranked pretty near the top. Every fight I win gives my master

77

status, a bit of which is passed on to me. Winning from you last time might sound good, but I know it meant little. I was there, remember?"

"Unfortunately, I can't forget," remarked Micah. "But I still feel somehow there's more to all this."

"That's enough for now. Let's get you out of here. Unless, of course, you have come to like this." One dark hand lifted Micah's flimsy embroidered tunic, revealing the shaved, sexless crotch.

Micah batted his hand away angrily.

Grir laughed as he got to his feet. "We will have two weeks to prepare. The performance will be part of the entertainment at the wedding feast of your mistress and Attlad."

"No!"

"You have no choice, you fool!"

"That's where you're wrong!" Micah shouted. "I have a choice! There's always a choice!"

"Surely. Live. Or die. That is a choice, yes? Is that what you mean?"

Micah clenched his hands into fists, his mind trying to sort through his rage and hurt and despair to the tactical aspect of his situation. How could he use this to his own advantage? One thing was clear; Attlad would be at the ceremony. He hadn't seen the man since that first humiliating night and had no idea how to find where he was. In order to retaliate, Attlad would have to be in striking range. Slowly his hands began to unclench.

"Perhaps you're right, Grir," he said quietly. "Perhaps in this instance, there really is no choice for me."

SIX

ne of the things Micah longed for most here in the Citadel, was to be outdoors again. He yearned for the open fields where he had learned to ride the wild Kudite horses; for the cliffs hanging over those distant mist-filled valleys, the spectacular views he had gazed at for hours from the rocky terrace outside Attlad's apartment back at the Complex. Day after day in the stifling confines of the Quarters was almost more than he could bear. Even when there were windows, they were apt to look out on an artificial scene, lit by artificial sunlight, and although it was very well done, the effect was to increase the oppressiveness of the place. By a great effort of will, he managed to rise above the constant humiliations, the games full of pain that all seemed to have as their purpose to emasculate and objectify him. But the lack of fresh air and strenuous exercise was something that threatened his very sanity. The more he thought about Grir's sudden proposal, the more it began to look like a life-saver.

The very act of passing through the gates of the

Quarters with Grir the first time, was itself a small thrill of triumph, although it didn't happen without incident.

One of the huge guards attached a small gold 'tracker disk' to his left tit. It was a simple procedure, but he dragged it out, squeezing on the nipple with one hand as he slowly pushed the metal clip through Micah's skin, enjoying the wince of pain that betrayed itself in his eyes.

"If you tamper with this disk in any way, you will be severely punished and all privileges will be revoked," he warned. "Same goes for the pearl belt. All the lady's boys wear them. It stays on."

Micah tried to argue this one, but without success. Wherever he went, he was to wear the pearl and gold girdle, hanging low on his hips under his tunic. His cock was pulled back and attached to it always, except when he was actually fighting. Grir had managed to gain him that one small concession.

The guards knew and respected the tall muscular fighter, joking with him as they locked or unlocked the doors to the Quarters each day. Apparently there was some serious betting on the outcome of the match, with Grir heavily favoured to win. Micah was out of shape, they said. He had spent too much time as a plaything of the ladies. It would not be likely he would be ready for a match, no matter what kind of a fighter he had been in his glory days as a Nebula Warrior.

All this he gathered from Grir, during the long walk through the Citadel to the fighter's Spartan apartment. Micah was curious to see what things were like outside, but he soon discovered there was no 'outside' as he knew it. The whole place was a warren of catwalks and iron stairways, with galleries running along the edge of the concrete canyons that comprised the buildings, like some gigantic tenement. It was almost impossible to see the sky and Micah now understood why the warriors from the Complex dreaded coming back to this cold unnatural place, so unlike the rough campgrounds they lived in for years at a time. The period of adjustment must be difficult. But at least these men had known what to expect, he thought bitterly, whereas to him it was all new and strange and terrible.

Talking with Grir, Micah soon discovered that it wasn't only the physical landscape that was cramped and twisted. Kudite customs were equally intricate and mired in tradition. Much of it made no sense to Micah, but he listened and filed everything away for possible future use.

"You say you're not a Kudite," Micah said one afternoon, as they sat cross-legged on the large wooden platform that was the 'relaxing area' of Grir's huge Spartan room. Opposite him, the naked alien's skin gleamed greenish in the pale light from the roof. "If you have as much status here as you claim, I don't understand why you are still a slave. Can't you just buy your freedom and go home, back to your countrymen beyond the mountains?"

"True, I'm not a Kudite, and I was not born a slave. I was a warrior, like you. I have a talent for fighting, and because of that, I gave up the right to bear children in order to strengthen me further. The Kudites do not understand such dedication," he added disdainfully.

Micah didn't understand it either, but decided not to comment on such a loaded subject as castration —especially self-chosen. "I still don't understand," he said cautiously.

"I cannot go back to my people. It is a disgrace to be captured, to be enslaved. So I stay. However, I cannot live here as a free man, because I am castrated. They see that as a condition only a slave would endure. I would be a second class citizen here no matter what I did, does that make it clear? It's easier to be a slave with status, than a free man whom everyone looks down on."

Micah nodded slowly. "Okay, I guess that makes sense."

"I couldn't own anything anyway, you see," Grir went on. "Men can only own property here by marrying a woman. They control ownership. Once you are married, you gain property status, even though you are not free to dispose of the property as you wish. A castrated man is not allowed to marry. None of it makes sense to me, either, but there it is."

"Yes," murmured Micah softly. "I think I am beginning to see." He was thinking of Attlad, the soldier, the leader of men with all that ambition driving him on. "Yes," he said again.

Grir smiled. "Thought you might be interested."

"So marrying is another way to gain status," Micah went on, thinking it through. "Why is owning property so important?"

"Only a man with property status can advance to be a Supreme War Lord, which I hear is what your former master lusts after, apparently even more than he lusted after you. And the lady, your owner, she will gain status by marrying a warrior. Both win, you see."

"And I lose," murmured Micah bitterly.

Grir shrugged. "It's all politics," he said casually. "Attlad and his brother have been fighting each other for years, I hear, each one trying to gain the upper hand. Unfortunately for Attlad, Kerdas doesn't play fair. Come on. It's late. I have to get you back before the fifth bell or they might not let you out again."

"Wait. What do you mean Kerdas doesn't play fair?"

"I mean that with the one it's merely a game of one-up-manship. With the other, it's hatred. Enough. We must go."

"Grir." Micah got to his feet and paused, not sure how to go on. "I just want to thank you for…this." He waved his arm to include the huge room, empty except for the weights and pulleys on the walls that formed part of their routines.

"There's no status in winning a match with a weakling," Grir said gruffly. "Come. It is time to go."

Micah looked forward eagerly to his time with Grir, the stark simplicity of the surroundings that resembled a gym more than they did living space, the easy comradeship of another warrior male, the familiar comforting smell of sweat and above all, that head spinning high of being pumped up.

One question about his companion that he had not yet found a way to ask, was answered one afternoon after they arrived and stripped down for their workout. Before taking up his position spotting Micah on the weight bench, Grir took down a grey box from a cupboard above the sink, sat down on the edge of the platform and opened it. He took out a syringe which he filled with liquid from one of a number of small bottles, and plunged the syringe into his thigh muscle. Micah couldn't help a small intake of breath.

"Surely you are not surprised?" Grir asked, his tone sardonic. "I have given up the natural male hormones my body makes on its own. It has to be replaced. At home we have kits supplied by the leaders. Here, my owner keeps me supplied."

"I wondered how your muscles have such bulk," Micah answered, but he felt uneasy. Was there something else in the syringe that could give Grir an unfair advantage? There was no way for him to check this out. "Have you ever lost a fight?" he asked.

"Not for a long time. I am the champion in my division. No one comes close." Grir rinsed out the syringe and put everything away again in the cupboard. "It will be good to fight a worthy opponent, even though I will win as usual," he added, with a dark grin.

"Not this time," Micah answered, but he wondered if any man would be able to overcome whatever synthetic drug was running through Grir's veins.

Up till that day, they had always followed the same route to and from Grir's place. That afternoon, Grir decided to take him back by a new route.

"Might as well see the sights, such as they are," he remarked, leading the way down a long iron stairway that clung to the edge of what looked like sheer rock. At the foot, he turned under an archway and they were suddenly in a beautiful garden filled with birdsong and sunshine. "It's all done with artificial light," Grir explained. "The sun never gets this far down, so they've set up a bank of lights to take its place. There are many of these small parks, the most a lot of people here ever see of nature."

"It may be produced by artificial means, but it's beautiful anyway," Micah admitted, looking around at the colourful display of flowers spilling down the sides of the rock, floating in a pool of water at the foot of a fountain that flowed from the next story up. The place was surprisingly empty, but he spotted a few single shapes moving close to the walls on the catwalks above them.

"Most people are still at their workplace," Grir explained, as if reading his mind. "It will be crowded here after the six bells have sounded. Come. This way."

Grir led the way up a series of twisting stairways to the catwalk two stories above, where he turned and started along the narrow bridge. Micah followed. He was looking down at all the colourful beauty below, when his eye was caught by a familiar figure striding along the catwalk one story down. Micah paused, his heart banging in his chest. For a moment it was hard to breath as he looked at the familiar broad shoulders and curly dark hair of Attlad. Then, his vision cleared as he saw another shape creeping along the wall behind his former master. Micah tensed. The shadow drew a knife. Micah cried out and leapt without thinking to the narrow walk twenty feet below.

It all happened very fast. The Terran landed off balance and almost fell to the ground, but his cry had alerted Attlad, who swung around and averted the blow. The knife sliced into Attlad's upper arm, drawing blood. Micah sprang forward with a roar of anger, his hands going for the attacker's throat. He didn't feel the blows raining down on his back and shoulders as he bent the man backwards over the railing and chocked the life out of him. With a final burst of strength, he flung the limp body over the side and turned to see soldiers approaching at a trot.

"Fool!" shouted Grir, suddenly at his side.

Attlad swung around as his name was shouted by the captain of the guard, and the next thing Micah knew, Attlad was in handcuffs.

"What the fuck is going on here?" cried Micah, stunned, as Grir dragged him off the bridge and through a small door into a dim corridor. He was too dazed to struggle.

"Shut up! What you just saw was Attlad being arrested for murder."

"What?? But *I'm* the one who killed the guy! Besides, it was self-defence! He was attacking Attlad from behind!"

"You're not asking the right questions, fool! Why were the military police right there, almost the instant it happened? Answer, it was supposed to happen, only you and I were not supposed to be there."

"A set up? Why?"

"Someone wants Attlad out of the way. Or at the very least, discredited. There could be any number of reasons, but Kerdas is at the top of the list of people who would benefit."

"That shit! Well, it isn't going to work this time! I can tell the police what happened. So can you."

"Chento, don't be a fool. You are a slave. So am I, for that matter. Nothing we say will carry any weight. We won't even be allowed in to see the Chief Magister."

"But we're witnesses!"

"Have you looked at yourself lately? You're wearing a short flimsy tunic and nothing else. Perfumed blond locks like a woman and a shaved crotch with no sign of a cock. You, my friend, are no longer a PB You are a pearlboy. Invisible. An object with no status. And they would say, quite rightly in my opinion, you are Attlad's heart slave, as well."

"What?"

"Technically, you may not belong to him any more, but you are still in love with your former master."

"No! You're wrong there, Grir. What happened just now was instinct, training. I would have done the same thing for you, or anyone who—"

"Shhh." Grir suddenly clamped a large hand over Micah's mouth as the sound of heavy marching feet reverberated through the air, making the metal bridges sing close to their hiding space. Micah struggled, wanting to go to them and demand to be heard, but Grir had caught him by surprise and now held him fast against the stone wall. There was no way he could extricate himself.

When the sound had died away and everyone had gone, Grir finally let him up. "Say nothing about this," he said. "Nothing! We will go on as if nothing has happened, until told otherwise. You understand?"

"I understand what you're saying, but I'll have to think about it."

"There's nothing to think about," Grir said crisply. "As far as they're concerned, we weren't even here."

But Micah *had* been there. He had seen it happen. He had automatically leapt to Attlad's defence. Now he had to find a way to discover what was really going on in the Citadel.

Micah went through the rest of the day in a daze, allowing himself to be strip-searched by the two new guards outside the Quarters, who took a long time thrusting their fat fingers in his hair, his mouth, his anus. He stood for hours beside his mistress, dressed in his absurdly short purple tunic that bared his smooth chest and gleaming tit rings, as she interviewed a delegation from another part of the Citadel, in her role as member of the Council.

At dinner time, Dadani took him to her private dining room, where she unclipped his cock and attached it to a blue silk ribbon which she tied to her chair. She tied his hands behind his back with another ribbon, this one so narrow it cut into his skin. She put some food into a bowl which she placed on the floor at her feet. She placed another bowl beside it, filled with wine. As she ate and drank with her guests, he was forced to bend over, his ass in the air, while he licked up his dinner like an animal, and tried to slurp up as much of the liquid as he could. Now and then she laid a hand on his head, running her fingers through his long blond hair. Halfway through the dinner, she casually pulled back his tunic, tucked it up out of the way and ran her hand over his ass as if checking it's smoothness.

"No matter what they do, they can't make his skin soft like a real pearlboy," she said sadly.

Micah gritted his teeth, no longer surprised that he was understanding more and more of what was being said. He did have the sense, however, not to react.

They left him there, tied by his cock to her chair while house-slaves cleared away the dinner and the ladies changed their clothes. His bladder was uncomfortably full, but there was nothing he could do about it.

About an hour later, she returned, bringing her sister with her. This was the first time since he had come to the Citadel that he had been singled out so much and it worried him. He was extra careful to obey all the rules. He drank the wine she fed him from a silver bottle, although he knew that soon he would have to piss, or his bladder would burst.

It was almost as if she read his mind. Her dark eyes danced with unaccustomed malice as she poured the wine mixed with water down his throat. He knelt at her feet, his tunic tucked up to expose his ass. Sure enough, his bladder soon began to ache with need. Not able to even hold his legs together to make it easier, his face eventually betrayed him.

"I think your boy needs to relieve himself," the sister said, glancing at Micah.

"He must say it himself," Dadani said. She untied his hands and looked at him severely.

"I need to piss," he signed at once, feeling like a small child.

"Do you know how, without breaking the rules?"

He hung his head and didn't answer, afraid she would insist on holding his cock for him, as the handlers did. Always he was forced to ask permission from one of the handlers, who enjoyed demeaning him by aiming his cock for him while he pissed into a hole in the floor, found in one corner of every room in the Quarters. He was, of course, not allowed to touch himself. "After the docking," they told him mirthfully, "you won't need us anymore. See how the boys do it?" Micah would push back the fear and disgust, trying not to notice the boys, whose little stubby cocks were always stiff. Urination seemed easy for them to accomplish without touching themselves, as they squatted over the small holes and relieved themselves without fuss. Micah was never allowed to forget what his fate was to be after his owner's marriage and the match with Grir that would be the entertainment.

Suddenly he felt her hand slap his ass smartly. "Answer me!"

"Yes, Lady."

"Show me. I find it hard to believe that such an untrained savage could do this well. And so we can be sure, I'll tuck this out of the way." She pulled up the front of the tunic, fastening it to the belt so that he was now completely naked below the waist. Then she untied one end of the silk ribbon and pointed to the appropriate corner of the room.

He got to his feet and began to walk. The ribbon trailed between his legs along the floor, forcing him to roll from side to side to avoid stepping on the thing. When he reached the corner, he started to bend his knees, but a clap made him turn his head.

"Face me," Dadani signed.

Micah obeyed. Using the wall as support, he bent his legs and carefully took aim, before releasing a hard stream of urine into the hole. The relief was so great, his legs trembled. He saw his mistress get to her feet, pick up a rod and walk towards him. He felt the hot flush of embarrassment as his cock drooped, dripping piss onto the floor. Almost at once he felt the sting of the rod on his ass and gasped in pain.

"Clean it up," Dadani said, her fingers barely deigning to make the signals.

He sank to his knees and licked up his own piss, the acrid smell of his urine clinging to the ribbon that trailed from his cock.

Later on, Dadani tired of the entertainment and called for more of her toys. Soon, Micah knelt naked on the floor, just one of a line of pearlboys who watched as Bar pleasured Dadani's sister. It was a grotesque sight, the boy's head hidden under the woman's long skirt, his little bare bottom rocking back and forth as he licked her. From time to time, she trailed a whip-like device over his skin, and as the metal tresses touched him, red and blue sparks crackled from it's tip and muffled cries came from under the long robe. After a while, the boy's pale flesh was spotted with angry red pin pricks. His body now moved in rhythmic jerks until at last, the cat dropped from the woman's languid hand and she lay back against the pillows, satisfied. Almost as an after-thought, she pushed the boy away from her.

Bar staggered out into the light, his face red and streaked with tears. Not even getting off his knees, he crawled over and took his place in the line-up. Locking his hands behind him, as was the custom, he looked straight ahead of him, like the others, his stubby cock erect in its circle of jewels.

Soon after that, the sister left, taking a few of the boys with her. Dadani dismissed the rest, except for Micah. Now that they were alone, Micah realized she had been hiding her true feelings in front of her sister. She sat back in her ornate carved armchair, piled with cushions, and stared at him, her dark eyes blazing with anger. Micah tensed, his hands clasped behind his back, chest thrust forward, knees apart. He wished she would do something, anything to break the tension. He sensed clearly that, once again, he was to be the whipping boy.

"Come here and stand before me," she signed at last.

He got to his feet and did as she ordered, his cock still hanging down, the damp, urine-soaked ribbon dangling from it to the floor. Dadani picked up the small, deadly whip with the sparkly tresses and swung it gently in the air. With the other hand, she signed, so he would understand her words, not realizing he got most of it anyway.

"You disgust me, slave. You're a symbol of something I now hate. Warriors!"

She lashed out at his cock with the whip. Micah screamed, and jerked back, as fire scorched through him.

"Stand still! Or do I have to chain you to the floor, like an animal?"

It would be easier to be chained, Micah thought, to be able to struggle against bonds, to express the agony stinging in his groin. But something inside made him accept the challenge. He raised his head and stepped back in front of his tormentor.

"Oh you're a real man, aren't you?" She laughed and lashed out at him again with such fury her whole body raised itself out of her chair. He was expecting it this time, but even so, the burning sting made his legs tremble. Again the lash cut into his unprotected groin, wrenching a muffled cry from him.

Dadani reached into the drawer again and pulled out a light silver chain. Leaning forward, she attached one end to the small ring at the tip of his stiffening cock. She ordered him to bend down, and as he did so, he saw the chain was actually shaped like a Y. Dadani clipped the other two ends to his nipple rings and signalled him to stand up straight. He grimaced with the pain as his tits were pulled down by his heavy cock, now held out in front of him, a perfect target for her lash. She smiled with satisfaction and stroked the small whip lightly along his shaft.

Micah moaned. Tiny shocks danced along his cock, making it jerk and bob against the chain, sending mingled pleasure/pain signals along his nerves. His tits stood out hard and aching.

Then she stopped. Surprised, he looked down to find her staring at his now rigid tool. Attlad's red dragon was plain to see, stretching toward her menacingly. He saw her eyes narrow, her mouth pull in. The whip came down strongly, aimed unerringly at the dragon's red eye near the tip of his cock. Micah screamed again and again as the assault on his manhood continued. Somehow, he managed to stay in place, though his legs trembled and his whole body convulsed as sweat poured down his sides. She only stopped when Kerdas came into the room.

"He has displeased you?" Kerdas asked casually, sitting in the chair next to hers and stretching out his long legs.

Dadani tossed the whip aside on the table between them. "He is a reminder of who he came from. If the giver of the gift is discovered to be worthless, the gift becomes worthless too."

Kerdas nodded.

"I know he's your brother, Kerdas, and I'm sorry things have turned out as they have."

"He has revealed his true colours," Kerdas said, or that's what Micah got from the words. "I have told you for years what Attlad is really like, how wild and uncivilized. Now he has killed a young civilian, and everyone knows the truth about him."

Micah stiffened. Could he have understood correctly? Was Grir right after all and Attlad had been set up? No matter how the man had betrayed him, this injustice could not be allowed to happen. On the other hand, he was standing here naked, a slave in an alien place. He didn't even know how to get out of the Citadel, never having seen the way in. When he concentrated again on what they were saying, Kerdas was comforting Dadani, leaning over with a caressing hand on her long dark curls.

"Later, Kerdas," she said, drawing away. "I must think about all this."

"The wedding ceremony?"

"There will be no wedding."

"What about him?" Kerdas motioned towards Micah.

She waved her hand dismissively. "Take him away," she said. "Do what you like. I don't want to see him again. He's a reminder of things I want to forget."

Micah saw the light of triumph in Kerdas's eyes and his heart sank. Dadani's torments had been bad enough, but there was no real calculation behind any of it. With Kerdas in total control, his life would be a living hell!

SEVEN

icah heard the sound of water, an irregular drip. Drip, drip. Plop, plop, plop. Drip. At first, he had been unaware of the sound. Nothing existed outside his world of agony. Pain flared through his body, exploding in his mind in unbearable brightness as Kerdas wielded the long snake-like whip that cracked in the dark air and stripped the flesh from his back. He had no idea of how long he had been in this secret torture chamber, His mind had ceased to operate. He had become nothing but his own exquisite suffering, until at last, he was left alone.

Now the insidious drip of the water buzzed in his head with maddening loudness. It was the only sound he could hear, since his head was encased in the thick darkness of a black leather hood. Through the layers of leather, the dripping water worked its way into his brain, a distraction that was at first welcome, but now threatened his sanity.

Micah hung from the ceiling from chains attached to manacles on his wrists. He was just able to touch the surface of two narrow blocks of wood, and his calves ached from the strain of standing on tip toe. His feet were held wide apart by a bar that fitted into the cuffs on his ankles. His balls were separated, tied tightly with a leather thong from which hung an iron weight. Kerdas had increased the weight, replacing it with a heavier one every half hour, or so, until he had tired of his exertions and left his new slave alone.

Micah had lost track of time, suspended in his tortured solitude, sweating in the darkness of Kerdas's secret cave beneath the Citadel. The cuts made by the whip stung as salt from his sweat seeped into them. He strained to hear any sounds of approaching footsteps, but all he could hear was the explosive intermittent splash of the water, drip dripping on the cold stone floor.

It seemed like a life-time since he had followed Kerdas's broad shoulders out of Dadani's rooms and through the interminable corridors that all looked alike. He had expected to be taken to the man's private apartments, but once they arrived there, Kerdas lifted a dark tapestry in the entry hall to reveal a panel that slid back out of sight at his touch. Kerdas led the way into a dusty little-used area and down a narrow stairway, cut in the thickness of the outer wall. The rough hewn stone grew cold under Micah's bare feet as they kept going down, down into darkness. Micah felt the tension build in his body. His cock strained against its chain, responding to the sweat he could smell from Kerdas, and that utterly masculine bulk. When they could barely see, Kerdas picked up a torch from a shelf as they passed, and lit it. Giant shadows leapt up the damp walls around them, showing moss growing along one side.

Finally, Kerdas paused and drew back a heavy leather curtain. He pulled Micah in after him and placed the torch in a sconce on the wall. Micah obeyed the signal to walk to the centre of the room, and looked around him. His heart hammered in his chest.

The chamber was more like a cave than a room. From what he could make out in the uncertain flare of the single torch, the walls were rough stone, hollowed out of the rock. The place echoed eerily. He couldn't see the ceiling. Micah felt the first touch of fear. He knew that no sound would escape from this hidden tomb to the Citadel far above. Kerdas could do what he wanted with him, here, and no one would ever know.

Why hadn't he turned on his captor then, Micah wondered now. Why had he allowed Kerdas to put him in chains and whip his writhing body until blood ran down his back and thighs, staining the stones below? Something he had pushed back deep inside himself had betrayed him — that longing for complete surrender to a strong male, unsatisfied since coming to the Citadel. It was an unspoken thing, an instinct that Attlad had seen in his soul and fostered until he needed it, craved it, could not feel complete without it. But his mind rebelled. Kerdas was not the man he wanted to master him, and now he suffered, fighting to keep from giving in, from letting Kerdas break him. Every time the whip curled around him, slicing a long red line through his skin, he pulled against his chains, swinging his body and increasing the pain on his balls.

Kerdas stripped down to nothing but a leather belt with a sort of jock strap, also of leather. Sweat glistened on his heavy shoulders, matting the black hair on his chest and stomach. He was built much like Attlad, but without the clear definition of muscle gained by an active life and many hours on horseback and in the gym, but the similarity was so strong, that Micah had to continually keep his mind from becoming confused. When Kerdas tired of dancing the whip over Micah's helpless body, he clamped weights to his already sore tits and without ceremony, rammed a metal butt plug up his ass. He laughed when Micah bucked against the pain. To the chain that still joined the tit clamps to Micah's cock, he added another length, going between his wide-spread legs to the ring on the end of the metal plug.

"Now you will dance and sing for me, Chento," he crooned, rubbing his crotch as he stood back and examined his victim. "I will break you, mighty warrior. My brother can't save you now! He can't even save himself!"

He picked up a square-shaped instrument from the box he had dragged from a corner and aimed it at Micah. When he hit the switch, a current raced from the ring in his cock, up the chains to his tits, leaping and dancing through the raised hard nipples till the whole pectoral muscle shook slightly. At the same time, Micah felt a hot jolt rush deep into his bowels. He cried out as the current got stronger, a long keening cry that wobbled in the air as his great body began to dance with pain. His own screams echoed and re-echoed, beating against his ears. When the charge stopped, as suddenly as it had begun, Micah still twitched and cried, his flesh still alive with the cruel energy, his feet scrambling to find a purchase on the small wooden boxes.

When he could see again, he understood why the pain had stopped. Kerdas had dropped the control box and was masturbating, both hands at work on his fat cock. His dark face was loose with lust and his eyes glazed, still fastened on his victim as he came.

After that, Kerdas lay back in the chair he had dragged from the shadows and played with his cock and balls for a while, watching Micah, taunting him, filling the vast cavern with his laughter. Micah couldn't look away, his eyes fixed on the man's heavy prick and low-hanging balls. His mouth was dry, his throat raw from screaming. Hatred of Kerdas burned in his gut like acid, yet he couldn't control his longing for the man. Micah knew Kerdas could see this in his eyes and this, too, was agony.

But Kerdas tired of this game, eventually. He lowered the chains holding Micah's arms, so the Terran sank to his knees. It was then that Micah realized he had urinated. The acrid familiar odour was almost comforting as he slumped on his knees in front of Kerdas.

"You are an animal," Kerdas told him, "and I will break you the way I break an animal. Do you understand?" He grasped a handful of Micah's long hair and yanked his head back, so he couldn't miss the signs. Micah tried to spit his defiance, but his mouth was too dry. Kerdas laughed. "I will give you a drink soon. When you are tamed."

That was when he took the leather cap out of the box and fitted it roughly over Micah's head, pushing the long hair up inside and fastening the hood closed with buckles at the back. There was a hole for his mouth and a narrow slit under his nose, but his eyes were covered. Only his ears were still exposed. His glistening chest heaved as he tried to steady his breathing, beating back the panic of utter vulnerability. Not being able to see where the pain would come from next, was terrifying beyond belief.

The chains rattled menacingly, then tightened. Micah struggled to get to his feet, to take the dead weight off his straining arms, but a blow to the side of his head knocked him off balance. Somewhere above him, he heard an engine whir into life, and he was pulled upwards into the air, muscles screaming in pain. As he rose higher, the weights dragging at his balls swung clear, shooting hot bolts of fire through him. His erect tits quivered in response, and his cock jerked to attention. Deep inside, the hard ridged edge of the butt plug moved against his bowels. Then the noise stopped.

In the ringing silence, his ears strained to compensate for the loss of his sight. He heard Kerdas moving about, but the disembodied sounds, coming from below, were disorienting and only filled him with fear. After the shock of all the pain he had endured, his brain was unable to process what he heard.

Then he caught the familiar swish of an object swinging through the air, one split second before a narrow wooden paddle hit the sole of his right foot. His whole body jerked with the force of the blow, sending pain everywhere as he hung helpless and naked in the damp air. Who would have imagined pain as intense as this could come from the tough sole of a man who had walked barefoot indoors and out for close to a year? Kerdas concentrated all his force on the right foot, until it felt as if on fire. Micah's nuts screamed in agony as the weights yanked the tender sacs, but all the time, his cock was rigid, pulling against the chain attached to his aching tits. Then Kerdas turned his attention to the left foot and reduced it, too, to a swollen centre of pain.

It took a while to realize that the blows had stopped. Behind his confining mask, Micah gasped for breath, tasting the leather and his own sweat and saliva. When he heard the engine again, he tensed. Nothing happened, though he could still hear the soft whir of well-oiled machinery. Then he felt the touch of cold steel against his burning feet. A bar. Suspended from the ceiling, as he was, but nonetheless providing some support, so he would not suffocate from his own weight. Gingerly, he rested his burning feet on the bar, gritting his teeth as his swollen flesh bore more and more of his weight. This new torture was more subtle than the rest, since he had to inflict it on himself in order to survive. Once he had found his balance and could breath again, he realized that the silence was complete. He stood perfectly still, swaying high above the ground on his painful trapeze, his ears straining into the darkness. Nothing. As the silence flowed around him, he knew that Kerdas had gone.

He began to sense textures to the silence, just as the darkness against his eyes pulsed with different shades of black. The silence blended with the shadows, becoming almost palpable, like the feel of the air touching his tortured burning flesh. His whole being was concentrated on working the pain through his body, one inch at a time, balancing the flaming heat of his swollen feet against the release of a bit of tension on his arm muscles. Survival became like a mathematical problem — how much stress could be born by releasing how much pain somewhere else — until the focus of his life was reduced to that rod of cold steel biting into his feet.

And then he became aware of the water, and another form of torture began.

Micah knew that it was very late, that he was exhausted, but every time he nodded off, in spite of the constant pain, he slipped off the bar and was jerked awake with a cry. His balls, which went numb from time to time, flamed into new agony. Sweat burst out again on his chest, shoulders, thighs, inflaming the cuts with new pain.

He heard footsteps and tension flooded him, making his muscles stand out even plainer on his sweat-soaked naked body. He knew Kerdas had a companion long before the men were in the room. They talked together so low that he couldn't make out the words. But when the engines started, he knew that he would soon be on the ground, and another phase of his torture would begin.

When the bar hit the stone floor, he sank to his knees, unable to stand. He could smell the wine and spices from the food the men had been eating and he realized how hungry he was. His mouth was dry with fear. Someone unbuckled the hood and pulled it off, taking a few handfuls of his hair with it. His eyes watered in the brightness of the torch-light as he stared up at Kerdas and his companion. Kerdas slapped him across the face with the back of his hand.

"Open your mouth."

Micah continued to stare, as if not understanding the order. The burly companion grabbed his head in an arm-lock and forced open his jaws. "This one needs a lot more training."

"I told you, he is an animal, like the man he used to service." Kerdas pulled out his fat cock and slapped it across Micah's face. "But I know what he likes," he said softly. "I know what my brother used him for, the only thing he's good for."

The smell of the man's cock was sweet to Micah, in spite of the hatred he felt towards him. His eyes glazed over with longing. It was weeks since he'd seen a cock like this, a cock almost like Attlad's great tool. Almost. He suppressed the whimper of desire that rose in his throat. But he couldn't control the jerking of his own cock, which was stiff and aching, reaching for this broad-shouldered man as if he real-ly had been Attlad.

Kerdas was quick to catch the look of need in the Terran's eyes, although it was instantly replaced with a defi-ant glare. "I promised you a drink." He thrust his cock into Micah's mouth, teasing it against the man's dry tongue and teeth, until it expanded even more. Just as Micah closed his lips around the swollen meat and began to suck, Kerdas pulled it out, and with a grim laugh thrust his whole cock down Micah's throat.

Micah gagged, fighting against the strong arms that held him. But it was useless. Part of him welcomed the tumescent flesh that filled his mouth, but part of him rebelled, fighting against the man who had betrayed his own brother. Just as he was about to lose consciousness, Kerdas withdrew. The cock was now slick with Micah's saliva, and as Kerdas hit him again with the rigid meat, it gleamed purple and dark red in the torchlight. Then, as Micah resigned himself to being brutally fucked in the face, Kerdas drew back and began to piss, in Micah's open mouth. Helpless to fight back, the slave swallowed desperately, trying not to choke on the hot acrid stream.

"That is the only liquid you'll ever get from now on, slave. Turn him over."

The burly man flipped Micah with ease, using the bar to hang him over, his swollen red ass presented to Kerdas like a gift. Micah gasped as his balls were grabbed and squeezed in a hard hand. The act set the trapeze bar moving, and his stomach heaved ominously as he swung helpless, head down, his long sweat-soaked hair trailing through the piss and blood and dirt. Then the butt plug was pulled out, leaving his hole gaping open, the pink shiny lips sucking at the cool air. Hard hands grabbed his hips, steadying him. Almost at once Kerdas's still rigid cock thrust in one great shove up Micah's screaming hole. Micah's hoarse cries egged him on, as his balls slapped against Micah's bleeding ass, over and over, thrust after agonizing thrust. All Micah was aware of was the battering ram of Kerdas's cock, twisting his guts with fire.

When Kerdas pulled away, his companion took his place, pumping into Micah with grunts of pleasure. He came quickly, leaning his considerable weight against the prone slave until he caught his breath and withdrew. Come drooled out of the distended red lips of Micah's hole.

"Prepare the chair. It's time we taught this scum that he is nothing, worthless, an object, not even a man. When we dock his cock, that will be plain. Every time he has to squat to piss, he will be reminded he is sexless. Every time he sees his tits getting bigger and bigger because his nuts no longer function, his he-man muscles melting into girlish curves, he will know what I have made him."

Micah wasn't positive of what he had heard, but he got enough of the meaning to make him almost faint. They would castrate him! Would modify his manhood so it was nothing but a useless pisser, like the pearl boys, who no longer could even fuck one another for their own pleasure. But he had no time to collect his thoughts, before he was dragged to a high backed chair. The seat was missing, and in its place, a ring of iron held a huge carved black dildo in place in the centre. It gleamed with grease in the light of the flaring torch, and Micah saw that its handle reached all the way to the floor.

"You will be stretched, so your ass will take anything and everything I please to jam into it. And you will be stuffed. All the time. You will no longer be able to do anything on your own. You can't eat, sleep, piss or shit without my permission. You are my thing, my trained animal. And I will bring you out for my special friends, like Ranlar, here, and you will be played with, like a new trinket. Women don't know what to do with a sex toy!" He laughed and shoved Micah into position over the carved cock.

One push, and Micah knew he would split in two, like an over-ripe melon. His thighs trembled as he squatted over the instrument, feeling the tip nudge his asshole open, his heart beating high in his chest, fluttering with fear.

But Kerdas didn't want to spoil his new toy. Not yet. He let Micah ease himself onto the giant thing, that pushed its way into his gut like a fist, although it wasn't that big. Micah heard his own breath rasping in his throat, escaping in little whimpers as his asshole stretched wider and wider, until at last, all of it was inside and his asscheeks rested in the metal frame of the chair. His balls swung in the air, still stretched by the heavy weight that almost touched the floor.

His hands were now manacled behind the back of the chair, his feet clamped in place to the chair legs. Another torch was lit, and Micah saw the points of light dance in the cruel depths of Kerdas's black eyes. There was a leather strap in his hands, and at first Micah thought he would be flogged with it. Instead, Kerdas fastened it around his neck, the ends attached to the high back of the chair like a garotte. Then Kerdas stripped before him and fed him his cock once again. Obediently, Micah sucked, taking it down his throat and swallowing the come, all but a small trickle that drooled over his chin.

Then he saw the razor in Ranlar's beefy hands. His eyes flew wildly from one to the other, and down to his own distended cock, still hard and unsatisfied, as it strained against its chain. His legs tensed as he tried to cringe back, away from the blade, and the dildo, moving against its iron ring, twisted deeper into his gut.

Kerdas saw the terror and laughed. "Not yet, boy. First we take away what makes you different here—that long blond woman's hair my brother paid so high a price for. I'll take it to him as a present. It will comfort him in his cell." And he laughed again, as Ranlar flashed the razor through the air with a flourish in front of Micah's face and drew it back in one smooth stroke, down the middle of his head. A long lock of blond hair fell into Kerdas's waiting hands.

Micah felt the tears well up behind his eyes. They were taking his personality away, reducing him to the cypher they wanted. A thing. He could feel his hair slide down his back and arms like silk, sticking to his sweaty thighs on its way to the floor. Then cold steel scraped over his scalp with a rasping noise, and in a few moments, he was utterly bald.

Kerdas ran his hand over the smooth surface with approval and Micah's naked scalp shuddered under his touch.

"It's crying," Ranlar remarked.

Kerdas laughed, and he walked away into the shadows. He returned with a box in his hands, which he placed on the floor out of Micah's range of vision. When he moved in front of Micah again, he held a long slender knife.

"If you know what's good for you, you'll keep real still," he signed.

Micah's breath was coming in gasps, his heart fluttering in his chest, as Kerdas drew the knife in a circle around first one nipple, than the other. As the steel cut through the skin, a thin red line welled up against the blade. "That's the part that will start to fill out like a girl," Kerdas said, and smiled. He began to slash shallow lines all down one side of Micah's chest and up the other, leaving a trail of bloody tracks, all about the same length. He took out his cock and rubbed the tip against the bloody marks, making patterns on the Terran's scarred chest. He tired of the game and made Micah lick his own blood of the knob of his cock. Casually he reached down, took a handful of salt from a box and rubbed it into the new wounds.

Then it seemed as if Kerdas lost patience, perhaps expecting more physical reaction to his random cruelty than Micah was giving. With a growl of fury he grabbed a whip that lay nearby and began to lash the helpless Micah repeatedly, his strokes falling in his shoulders, his legs, even his face. Micah writhed under this attack, which worked the dildo more cruelly inside him. Soon his gasps turned into screams, and then hoarse nameless wails, as his skin burst into flames.

When Kerdas tired, Ranlar unshackled Micah and pulled him off the chair, the phallus still up his ass. Micah collapsed into the floor, where he was hog tied and hosed down with a pail of water. Ranlar took hold of the dildo handle and pushed it up and down, watching the exposed pink lips of Micah's anus stretch wide and suck in and out around the slick wood with a slurping sound. Micah's eyes glazed over, as his cock responded, sticking up as stiff as possible and tugging against its restraint.

"That will have to be fixed," Kerdas remarked, watching. He went to the box and came with a small padlock which he slipped through the ring at the base of Micah's cock, then through the ring at the tip, so that the shaft was bent almost double. "You are not allowed to have pleasure," he said. "This will take care of it till the operation. And this," he went on, taking a tube from the box, " will keep you from pissing without permission, as you did before."

Micah squealed like a wounded animal as the tube was forced into the slit of his cock, and fastened with a clip. Even if he did try to urinate, the flow would be stopped. Ranlar thrust his shaved head back into the hood, and as a final touch, a leather dildo was shoved down his throat and fastened in place like a gag.

"Remember, you are nothing without me. You can do nothing, feel nothing, see nothing. All you can do is pray for me to remember you now and then."

Satisfied, Kerdas doused the torch and walked away with his companion, leaving the Terran naked on his back, his legs splayed helplessly apart, his asshole stretched wide with the dildo and his mouth crammed with leather. Even his piss-slit was sealed.

Micah lay in the dark, the stone floor cold against his aching back, and cursed Kerdas in his mind. Even though his head was covered with the hood, it was cold, deprived of the luxurious covering of hair he was used to feeling.

At first he concentrated on breathing through his nose, on not gagging on the long leather phallus that filled his mouth. Then he became aware once again of the drip, drip of the water. How could he have not noticed it for so long?

But after a while, even this torture receded, as his bodily functions demanded his attention. Alas, he no longer had the power to do anything about them. His bowels could churn into cramps, his bladder fill, and he could do nothing but suffer.

At last he realized that Kerdas was right. All he had left to hope for was that Kerdas would return soon, that Kerdas, the man who controlled him completely, would not forget his existence.

EIGHT

icah's world of pain and darkness gradually took over his brain, leaving little room for rational thought. His life became a succession of dark islands where numbness would creep over him at last, only to be rudely shaken off by an unseen tormentor.

The first time he heard the footsteps, he knew it wasn't Kerdas and tears leaked out behind his covered eyes. He had been waiting for so long! Now he was afraid there would be no relief for him. Boots tramped across the stone floor, pausing at his side. Micah whimpered.

"You want to piss?"

Micah nodded vigorously, rocking his whole body in his efforts to communicate his need. His mind was so numb it didn't occur to him that he was responding to a spoken question for the first time. He heard clothing being adjusted and a sharp sting of urine hit his ass, stinging the welts and cuts there. Micah squealed as a boot hit the dildo, sending shock waves through his tormented body.

Then a large hand descended on his cock and pulled out the plug, releasing a stream of hot piss that arced onto Micah's chest. The relief was so sudden it was painful. He was helpless to control his own cries.

He got used to never seeing his keepers. They came at irregular intervals, though it was hard for him to keep track of the passage of time. They pissed on him, fed him their cocks, pulled out the dildo and allowed the shit to pour out of him on the floor, leaving him to lie in his own excrement. Sometimes, another man would arrive and hose him down, make him crawl around the cavern, still blind in his hood, and beat him with a paddle until his ass felt swollen to twice its size. "Kerdas likes a nice hot ass," the man would say, and laugh at his own wit. He made Micah kneel and suck his cock, before he was allowed to suck a bottle with a huge cock-shaped tit. His meal was always the familiar liquid protean. He knew there was piss mixed into it. "A gift from Kerdas," he was told, "so you won't forget him."

They tied him spread-eagled to a latticed frame, his balls hanging down, weights suspended from them. Another time they shackled him the wall for three feeding periods. They tied him to a whipping post one time and beat him fiercely, because some shit had squeezed its way out around the dildo. A bigger dildo was then forced up his ass. He never knew when some new horror would be done to him, or when.

One time several men came clattering into the cellar. They didn't speak to each other or to him. Hearing the boots ring on the stone floor was chilling. They untied him and yanked him to his feet, where he tottered a moment, getting his balance. Abruptly, the dildo was pulled out of his ass.

Hold it in," one of the men said. "Hold it all in."

Micah nodded, desperate to do exactly what he was told. The tube was jerked out of his piss slit. He shuddered, feeling the hot piss ready to spill out.

"Hold everything in," the man repeated.

Micah tensed every muscle in his body in the effort to obey, as they led him across the floor. They lifted him up to a wheel he hadn't seen before and fastened him there on his back, arms and legs stretched wide. One of them unstrapped the gag and removed it. The rubber cock-tit was pushed in and he sucked hungrily, grateful for even this respite.

Then, just as the bottle was pulled from his mouth, the wheel began to spin. It was so unexpected, it terrified him. He had been braced for pain, but this sudden dizzying spin threw his whole world into chaos. A scream rose in his throat, and with it, the liquid he had just eaten. Vomit dribbled out of his mouth and he lost control of his clenched muscles. Piss streamed into the air flying out behind him, shit splattered through the spokes to the stone floor. The wheel spun on and on, and the naked shaved man tied to it gasped and chocked in his humiliation, his pain rising to a thin hopeless wail in the darkness.

As the wheel slowed, the first strokes of the whip hit his cock. His mouth stretched wider, trying to crank up his screams, but the gag was shoved back in and only drool managed to slide out around the shiny leather. The beating went on and on, until he lost consciousness.

When he came to, he knew he was alone. He was still tied to the wheel, but something was different. After a while, his fogged head cleared enough for him to realize they had not replaced the tube in his piss slit. His asshole was empty, too. He found this frightening. The distended lips of his anus hung in the air, sucking helplessly at emptiness, needing to be filled. Tears slid out of his eyes, dampening the leather that covered his face. The only signs that

Kerdas remembered him now, were the welts and bruises pulsing on his body. The odd idea formed in his mind that he should try to control his bodily functions, just as if he was still plugged with the catheter and the dildo. If he could manage not to piss or shit, maybe Kerdas would be pleased with him, and would forgive this disgusting display.

Micah hung on to this idea, and for a while it was easy, since there was little liquid left inside his body. But as time passed, the inevitable need built up again. It became more and more difficult to hold back, knowing there was nothing physically stopping him. Still, he persevered. His cock with its widened piss slit gaping in the air, became his total focus. Slowly he gained a little pride in his achievement.

But Kerdas didn't want him to have any pride. He must have known what Micah would try to do. He must have timed it, waiting until it was impossible and Micah lay once more with his own urine on his chest and stomach. Defeated. Again.

This time when the men came, Micah didn't try to think. He let them pull him off the wheel, walk him around on his rubbery legs then stop, as another man came in. Micah's hood was pulled off and he blinked in the bright torch light. He made out Kerdas, standing in front of him, a leather cat in one hand. At once, he dropped to his knees.

"You couldn't control yourself, could you?" Micah hung his head. "Animal!" Kerdas lashed out at him, the long tresses of the whip wrapping around Micah's flaccid cock. "You will learn. You will learn to piss only when I give the word; shit only when I say so."

Kerdas pulled out his cock. He backed up a few steps, making Micah crawl after him, his mouth open, drooling at the prospect of liquid of any sort. When Kerdas stopped, Micah took the cock in his mouth hungrily, sucking greedily. Then Kerdas released a stream of hot urine down

Micah's throat. The slave gulped it down, desperate not to spill one drop. Kerdas motioned to the other two men, and Micah drank their piss, too. When all the men were dry, they forced bottles into his gaping mouth, and Micah swallowed the strange combination of liquids they contained. He didn't stop to analyse what they might be, aware only that Kerdas and his whip must be obeyed.

After this, they clipped a long thin leash to the ring at the base of his cock. One of the men stood in the centre of the chamber, holding the other end, while Kerdas whipped Micah until he ran blindly around and around in a circle, never able to escape the lash. When he was finally allowed to stop, Kerdas gave him the order to piss. At once, he started to urinate.

"Not like a man! Like the pearlboys!"

Still pissing, Micah squatted on his haunches and emptied his bladder on the floor, hardly noticing the hot liquid that spilled over his bare feet.

Kerdas grunted in satisfaction. "Clean him up and bring him upstairs in an hour. I think it's time to show him off."

Micah now had a shiny black leather collar around his neck and a brass ring around his cock. His head was freshly shaved and a ball gag stretched his mouth wider than he had thought possible. He knelt on a table, his ankles and wrists clamped to the metal. His legs were wide apart, his ass high in the air, his balls hanging free. A man he had never seen before inserted a long needle into his balls and began to inject something into him. Sweat broke out in a thin sheen all over Micah's taut body. Was this part of the operation that would make him sexless? Or were they going to have some fun with him first? The big needle had some kind of attachment at one end, and a tube leading to something out of his line of vision.

His balls were expanding. It seemed like half an hour or more, but finally the needle and its attachment were taken away. Micah's balls felt monstrous by this time, filling the space between his legs like a giant gas ball. When he was made to stand, it was awkward and painful to move. He also found it made his cock look small by comparison. The man who had done this to him, bent him over the table and fucked his ass, banging hard into the huge thing with evident delight before he came.

Micah heard Kerdas's voice as he stood up and turned around. After so much time in the dark, his eyes had still not adjusted completely to the brighter lights here in Kerdas's private apartments. Kerdas was holding a silver sphere in his hand as he looked down at Micah, forced to stand with his legs wide apart to accommodate the thing. He sneered. Micah blushed, seeing how small his cock looked, standing rigid, yet only a tiny round nub in the middle of this huge shaved monstrosity.

"I thought your last night as a man you should have a real treat," Kerdas said. "Give you real balls, giant-sized he-man balls you can dream about later when you have none at all." He tossed the silver sphere back and forth, from one hand to another. "And this is for you, too. I want you to carry it for me, but if you drop it, you'll be thrown back downstairs and forgotten. Do you want that?"

Micah shook his head, the sweat dripping down his sides even though the room was much warmer than he'd been used to in the cellar.

"Turn around and bend over."

Micah obeyed, steadying himself by holding onto the edge of the table as Kerdas pushed the hard metal sphere up his ass. Micah whimpered as the ball forced its way past the ring of muscle. Once inside, the sphincter clamped around it, holding it deep inside.

"At the end of the evening, if it is lost, so are you. Do you understand?"

Micah nodded. A slap on his ass told him it was time to stand up and follow Kerdas into the other room. Then, as an afterthought, Kerdas pointed to the pearl and gold belt Micah still wore and said something to one of the men. With a snip of powerful cutters, the chain fell to the floor at the slave's feet.

"Follow me," Kerdas motioned, and went through the heavy embossed curtain into the room beyond.

Micah walked awkwardly, almost bowlegged as he struggled to accommodate his bloated sac. The room next door was dimly lit, the floor strewn with cushions and low tables. Several men reclined naked, laughing and talking languidly among themselves. Some of them smoked an intricate water pipe. In the middle of the room was a large wrought iron cage on wheels, and inside, a pale hairless creature lay curled in a fetal position on its side.

"Let it out," Kerdas said, and picked up a small whip with a carved ivory handle. "It needs some exercise." One of the pearlboys Micah didn't recognize rushed to the cage and swung open a door at one end. "Watch and learn," Kerdas said to Micah. He cracked the whip in the air, the end just touching the reddened ass of the creature, who began to lurch frantically around the room on all fours. A string of coloured balls hung from its ass, bouncing along on the floor as it scuttled by. Micah stared in horrified fascination. Slowly he took in the details; the smooth crack of the ass, totally free of scrotum and testicles. When the creature stopped and squatted as ordered, there was nothing between the legs but a barely discernable knob with a wide piss slit, that gaped like a damp red mouth, its lips slightly parted.

The soft hairless body had no muscle definition, and the tits with their large black rings, stood out hard about one inch above small soft breasts.

He is showing me what I am to become, Micah thought in horror, and a hot wave of pure rage rolled through him for the first time in a long while. The rage steadied him and cleared his head. He knew he had to escape that night. He looked around the room again. The men laughed, as they smoked, their pupils dilated, their movements slow and languid. The pearlboy now lay between the legs of one of them, the man's soft cock held gently in his mouth. Compared to the creature squatting patiently before them, the boy looked quite masculine.

Kerdas placed his boot on the creatures shaved head and shoved. As the body folded to the ground, he grabbed the green ball at the end of the string and gave it a jerk. A thin cry escaped as the string pulled a red ball, then a blue one, then yellow one, out of the distended anus. Each one was bigger than the one before. On Kerdas's command, the pale sweating body struggled up on all fours, presenting the reddened ass, cries-cross with welts, to Kerdas for more punishment. With a sudden growl, the man yanked the rest of the balls out of the poor creature. A high unearthly scream wailed around the room. The bright spheres lay on the floor, glistening with mucus, a colourful rosary of pain. Micah stared as the red anus gaped open, turned almost inside out. He felt his cock stiffen against his will, standing out like a small thumb in the middle of his inflated scrotum.

"Soon you will have a fine matched set, Kerdas," one of the guests cried, indicating Micah. He fell backwards with laughter at his joke.

Micah shifted his weight, the bloated balls throwing off his balance. He watched Kerdas hook a thumb in the creature's mouth and open it impossibly wide, and he saw there were no teeth left inside, nothing to graze Kerdas's fat cock as it slid down the willing throat without obstruction. For a moment, Micah's stomach heaved. He felt his anus pulse. Just in time he clenched down, holding the metal sphere in place. If he was to escape, he mustn't alert anyone here to his resistance, by disobeying an order.

The evening continued, and Micah was made to run around the outside of the room, while they all slapped at his great bloated sac. Then Kerdas told him to stand in front of the creature's open mouth.

"Show our guests how well-trained you are," Kerdas said, leaning back on the cushions. "Piss. Now."

Micah let go at once, and a trickle of urine hit the poor thing's face and was lapped up quickly. A few of the men laughed, but Micah sensed that they had exhausted themselves before he had been brought in. He thought it likely the whole thing had been set up more to terrify him than to amuse the guests. He was not surprised when Kerdas ordered his trusted handler to take Micah back downstairs.

"Prepare him for the knife. We will proceed with the alterations as soon as the medic gets here." He lay back on the mound of cushions and pulled his sex toy close, using the ring pierced through its belly button.

Micah lowered his eyes and followed the handler out to the entrance hall and through the hidden door to the steps that led into darkness. Over the course of that bizarre evening, his thoughts had become more and more focussed, fuelled by anger and the certain knowledge that this was his only chance to escape. Now he felt as clear and rational as the Nebula Warrior he used to be, before a combat mission.

The handler, dressed casually for these 'unofficial' duties doing Kerdas's secret dirty business, obviously had no thought of Micah as a person. He never even glanced behind him to make sure the slave was following. As they continued down the smooth stone steps, Micah paused for a moment, reached behind and caught the steel ball as his muscles expelled it from his asshole. Then he moved further down the stairs, waiting until they were almost at the bottom before he made his move.

"Halt!" Micah's strident command bounced off the walls like the crack of whip.

Startled, the man turned, his jaw dropping open in alarm.

Micah swung back his arm and hurled the small, but deadly missile at the handler's head. The man went down with a grunt, hit square on the temple. Micah was on him almost at once, and finished him off with one powerful blow to the throat. Grunting with effort, he stripped off the man's clothes and boots and got into them himself. The pants were loose, but even so, his bloated scrotum rubbed painfully against the rough material. He would have to walk slowly and with great care. Luckily, the boots were almost the same size. Once dressed, he pulled the naked body into the farthest dark corner of the cave.

His plan unfolded in his mind as he went along. He knew he had to avoid the Quarters completely, since everyone there would recognize him. There was only one place he could go, one person he could turn to, and he had no certainty that Grir would offer help. He wasn't even sure he could find his way outside from this section of the Citadel. Determined to make the effort or die in the attempt, he doused the torch in the puddle of water next the body, and made his way back to the secret entrance.

High pitched squeals came from the inner room of Kerdas's apartment as Micah slid soundlessly across the tiled floor to the door. He froze. For one blinding moment, he was possessed of such rage that he wanted to burst in there and put an end to the poor creature's suffering, but common sense told him this would be suicide. He would be very lucky to save himself. He went out into the corridor, closing the door soundlessly behind him.

It was very late. There was no one about and Micah walked as quickly as he was able in his present state, keeping as much in the shadow as possible. He was always aware that he had no hope of passing unnoticed, if anyone saw him. His shaved head would give him away. Speed was his only hope, since he knew the house-slaves were up early, preparing the public areas for the day. But the corridors looked all alike to him, and he had only come this way once, a time that seemed hazy and confused after the treatment he had been through.

He turned to the right and walked for about ten minutes, before he realized to his horror that he was near Dadani's garden, with its turquoise pool. He turned away, then paused. Maybe he could find something there to put over his head as a makeshift cover. He remembered how Dadani and her friends often left things lying around, and the house-slaves would not have been there to clean up yet.

Cautiously he crept through the gates into the enclosed garden. No lights shone from any of the windows and the peaceful air of the place calmed his jittery nerves. The waterfall called to him, reminding him of the stench that must be on his scarred body. He examined the grass, finding a few uneaten fruits and several goblets of wine, which he finished quickly. But there was nothing but a green cloth that trailed over a bench, obviously left by one of the women. Wrapping that around his head would make things even worse, he decided, but at least he could use it as a kind of loin cloth, to swaddle his aching genitals.

Seduced by the gentle murmur of the water, he stripped off his stolen clothes and stepped under the soothing spray. It was heaven to feel the cleansing waves wash over him, even though the coolness stung his welts and the more recent open cuts made by Kerdas's whip. He was just bending over to pick up his tunic, when he saw a shadow and tensed, ready to spring.

"Chento?" The voice was a mere whisper on the fragrant air.

"Bar." Micah straightened up, still ready for attack. He studied the boy's face in the moonlight for anything hidden behind the pleased expression.

"Did Kerdas give you back?" Bar signed.

Micah shook his head. "You should go back to the Quarters, Bar. Don't mention you've seen me."

"You are going to escape?" Bar asked at once. "You can trust me, Chento. I would never give you away."

"Thanks." Micah continued to get dressed, very self-conscious when he saw Bar looking at his balls.

"That will go back to normal size," Bar said, indicating the balloon between Micah's legs. "It will take several hours, I'm not sure how long exactly."

"That's good to know."

"Use this to put over your head." He took off his own tunic, which was, at least, a purple so dark it could pass as a head covering late at night.

"Do you have anything of value?" Bar went on, barely acknowledging Micah's thanks.

Micah shook his head.

"I will give you one of my pearls."

"Bar, I don't think those decorations on the boys' belts are very valuable, but thanks for the thought."

"That's not what I meant." Bar drew him into even deeper shadow. "I mean one of these." He took Micah's hand and laid it against his hard little scrotum, separated by its silver and blue beaded cage.

"I don't understand," Micah signed. The thoughts he was having were too far fetched to be real.

Bar looked away for a moment. When he looked back, Micah saw the shimmer of tears in his eyes. "I will do anything for you," Bar said. "I will give you a knife and you can cut open one of these sacs and slide out the pearl you will find there—"

"Wait! Do you mean there's an actual jewel in…."

Bar nodded. "That's the real reason they call us pearlboys. It's our dowry, for when we go back to the temple. But I want to give one to you."

"Bar, I can't accept this."

"But—"

"There's no time! Besides, it'd be pretty obvious, don't you think? I'm no surgeon! You might even bleed to death!"

Bar drew away, obviously hurt. Micah reached out and pulled him close and kissed him slowly, tenderly, probing his mouth softly with his tongue.

Bar's fingers spoke against his neck. "I'll never forget you. Good luck!" Then he pushed away and vanished into the shadows.

Micah found his own eyes were suspiciously damp. Blinking in annoyance, he wrapped the tunic around his head like a hood and walked out of the garden. Too late he wished he had asked Bar for directions.

NINE

o moonlight penetrated the dense night. The catwalks and galleries and bridges connecting the different levels of the Citadel cris-crossed around him, all but invisible except for the ghostly glow of tiny blue lights that outlined each narrow footpath. The effect made the scene resemble some spectral space station, floating in the black void.

It was only his soldier's instinct that guided him through the eerie maze. Those daily walks to and from Grir's Spartan rooms were embedded in his memory; so many paces to the right, a turn to the left and immediately up the ladder to the catwalk two levels above. The metal steps thrummed under his careful tread. It was very late. Except for two drunken men singing together on a gallery below him, he had seen no one.

Apparently it was not the custom to leave lights on out-side doors or at windows this late. It occurred to him there might even be a law against being out at this hour. He carried a short metal bar in his right hand, pried off the grating of an air shaft he had passed on the way. Every now and then his foot stumbled against some irregular bump in the walkway and his heart thumped painfully at the dull reverberation. He crouched for a moment, tense, his ears straining. Then he went on, cursing his swollen, bruised balls that made moving around just that much more difficult.

Like all the rest, Grir's door was shrouded in darkness. If Micah hadn't known it was there, he would have walked right past it. Softly he lifted the latch and pushed. Nothing happened. He felt along the side of the wall until he found the air vent he had noticed to the right of the door. It was circular in shape, and just large enough to force his way through, once he pried off the grate. In spite of what he had been through recently, the muscles were still powerful, and it took him only a few moments to accomplish his task, using the metal bar effectively. Carefully, he removed the circular unit, placed it against the wall and used it as a step to climb up and into the hole. He paused, crouched in the open space as he gathered himself for the spring to the floor, the bar held in his right hand. At the last moment, he thought he saw a pale shadow move, slightly to his left. He leapt, twisting his body in that direction. His knee connected with bone. In an instant he was astride a naked man, pressing the bar against his throat. He couldn't see any features, but he knew this slight figure wasn't Grir.

A torch flared close beside him. "If you hurt him in any way, you are a dead man." Grir's voice was low, menacing.

Micah pressed tighter against the man's throat. He was pale, his shoulder length hair almost white in the torchlight, but his face was young. The eyes staring back at him with amazing calm, were pale green. He didn't try to struggle. Whoever he was, he obviously mattered to the fighter.

"I need your help, Grir," Micah said, not moving his eyes from his prisoner.

"No. I will report you to the authorities. After I kill you."

"Won't that bring suspicion on you," Micah said, "killing a man you were scheduled to fight? Maybe they'll think you're losing your edge, Grir." He forced his victim's head back just a little farther. The man's eyelids began to flutter.

"The match is off. Now you are nothing."

"I am a slave, like you. Doesn't that mean anything? Or didn't you learn a thing from your Terran lover?"

"I learned that we speak different languages. Let him go. He's losing consciousness."

"First, your promise."

Grir made a guttural noise of disgust. "Yes. I promise."

Micah pulled back the bar and got to his feet.

"Hell and damnation!" Grir's voice bellowed suddenly. "You are a fool! Moron!" He must have run out of English vocabulary, because he then broke into the liquid gutturals of the Kudites for a few moments.

Micah thought he was shouting at his companion, until Grir suddenly grabbed Micah's tunic and ripped it open. Micah raised his iron bar to defend himself, but Grir casually tore it from his hands and tossed it across the room. "You will ruin me!" Grir shouted, and tugged at the small metal tracking disk embedded in Micah's left tit.

"Shit! I forgot about that!"

"Obviously," remarked Grir contemptuously. "You do not think like a Nebula Warrior, do you? You are the one who is losing his edge."

"It's been a while."

"Don't move." Grir strode away into the shadows and came back with a small cylinder. "After what you have probably been through with Kerdas, this will be nothing," he remarked, placing the cylinder against the disk.

Fire cut into Micah's nipple. He swallowed the scream that rose in his throat. His hands began to shake. He saw that Grir was naked, his black-green body shining in the torch-light. The beauty of his muscles distracted him from the pain briefly.

Grir moved away and held the charred disk over the flame until it was nothing but a twisted blob. He seemed oblivious of the intense heat against his own fingers.

"Thanks." Micah adjusted his tunic.

"I am merely protecting myself. Now, I will replace the vent. When I come back in, you will leave. You have put me in enough danger."

"You promised—"

"You are a bloody fool!" Grir marched out the door, naked as the day he was born, and proceeded to replace the vent.

"So much for the idea of honour among slaves," muttered Micah, helping the young man to his feet. He, too, was naked, but Micah didn't have much time to admire him before Grir was back.

"All right, one hour," Grir said. "You have one hour, then you leave, or I report you, and that's a promise!" He turned and marched into the shadows. Even in his anger, Micah appreciated the hard muscular ass and the heavy thighs.

"What about your friend?" he called out after him.

"What Jaylun does is his own business."

Micah turned to see Jaylun coming towards him carrying a jar of ointment. He stopped in front of Micah and smiled as he drew back the tunic to reveal the ravaged nipple. He was small compared to the giant Grir, but his muscles were long and well defined like a swimmer's. His pale hair fell around his face as he worked over Micah's chest, applying the salve to the burning tit, and then to other cuts and welts his gentle fingers sought out. When he was finished with the chest, he motioned for Micah to sit on the stool, pulled off the shirt completely and went to work on his back.

It was a soothing experience to have someone care for him again, and the feeling he got from this man was definitely one of caring. Gradually he felt his muscles unknot, his breath come easier. His mind relaxed.

"Hope I didn't hurt you," he said when the young man was finished and sat down in front of him on the floor.

Jaylun shook his head and raised his hands to sign. "I do not understand your language. Do you feel better now?"

Micah nodded. "Do you agree with him that I can only stay one hour?" he signed.

"Yes. But I understand more of what is going on here than he cares to find out about. These are my people, Chento. You and Grir are both outsiders, especially you. He told me about you saving the man's life, and how that man is now accused of murdering the one you killed to save him.

"I wanted to go to the authorities and tell then what really happened. Grir held me back and now it's too late."

Jaylun rose to his feet and went over to a shelf on the wall. He seemed perfectly at ease in his nakedness. When he turned, Micah saw the docked cock curled against the small hard little balls. So, he was a pearlboy, or he had been one. He seemed older than the boys in the Quarters. Jaylun came back with bread and some sort of fruit squares, which Micah ate greedily, thankful for the food. Jaylun sat quietly beside him, sipping juice from a metal bottle.

"I must get out of the Citadel," Micah signed. "Maybe if I can get back to the people who know me at the Complex, they will know how to help Attlad. Can you show me how to get out of this labyrinth?"

Jaylun nodded slowly. "I could, but there is another way." He paused. "You were this man's P.B.? His love slave?"

Micah flushed. "He tossed me aside, gave me away to Dadani. Didn't Grir tell you about that, too?"

"That was not the lady's idea. Kerdas told her to demand you as her bonding gift. She did not want you particularly, but he persuaded her it would be a great test of his intentions as future husband."

Micah stared at his pale companion. "How do you know all this?"

"I am a recorder for the Council. Dadani is a Counsellor. So is Kerdas. Besides, there is always talk on the pearlboys' network. I still hear what is going on. That's how I knew Kerdas had finally got his hands on you, although this was only unconfirmed rumour," he added.

So it was Kerdas all along. Micah thought for a moment, staring ahead of him, unseeing. "What is the other way of helping you mentioned?"

"You would be able to testify for Attlad if you had enough status to give you credibility. So far, Kerdas has seen to it you have been robbed of everything. However, you can go to the Cave of Truth. If you pass their tests, you will show them the truth through the clouds of doubt—"

"Hold it! Are you talking about reality, or is this all symbolic?"

"Both. It is a real cave. And the tests are real. The rituals are old, concerned with removing all the outer veils that cloud the mind and seeking the pure vision found in dreams."

"Like Attlad's father," Micah said, remembering the incident at the Complex.

"Yes. He is one of the vision dreamers. In this case, his voice is silenced, because of his close connection with the accused man. You, however, could be heard, if you make it through the rituals."

Micah looked into Jaylun's pale eyes. "You believe in all this magic, don't you?"

"It is part of my life," Jaylun said simply. "Grir can not understand. His people are less… complicated."

"For once I agree with Grir," Micah remarked. "So my choices are: I stay here and get turned over to the authorities, which means Kerdas would eventually kill me. Or, you give me a map and I try to get out of here, cross the damn desert I know separates the Citadel from the Complex and then try to convince a bunch of soldiers their leader needs saving, if, by that time, it isn't too late. Or, I go through this magic ritual, with a slim chance I will then be believed."

"You are a strong man. The chances are good."

Micah thought of his days and nights of torture at the hands of Kerdas and his minions, and was glad of the strong trained physique that might save him yet. "Lead on. What do I do now?"

"Wait here. I will get dressed and then I will take you."

"What about Grir?"

"I do this for him as much as you. There is little chance of your trail leading anyone back here if you are with me. As you have already noticed, I was a pearlboy. I was brought up in the temple and know all the underground tunnels and chambers as well as I know Grir's two rooms here. Because of my studies, I also know the Cave of Truth. Some day I may be there myself, but I have far to go before reaching that stage." He stood up and looked at Micah consideringly. "You will need a hood," he signed. "I will be back."

He disappeared into the shadows, moving as if he knew the area well, as no doubt he did. Micah trusted him, which was odd, considering he didn't trust Grir at all. The gentle

Kudite, however, was a special kind of person, Micah realized. He wondered how he and Grir had ever gotten together.

Ten minutes later, Micah and Jaylun stole out of the house and disappeared into the night. Micah had not seen Grir again, nor heard any murmuring talk between the two men, but he well remembered the silent conversations he used to have with his master, Attlad, fingers touching flesh, talking directly without sound. Jaylun had supplied him with a cloak with a hood, a bag filled with bread and fruit, a coil of rope and a small automatic torch.

They went up steps, across several catwalks and down a long ladder until they reached the lowest level. Above them in the layered darkness, Micah sensed the towering oppressive canyons of the Citadel. They walked for a while in silence, the only illumination the faint glow from the blue guide lights. At last, Jaylun led the way through a low arch into a deserted courtyard. Even in the daytime, little light would penetrate this far down. Jaylun reached for his hand and led him over some large broken fragments of masonry to a grate that loosely covered a culvert.

"In here," he signed, his fingers tracing the words on Micah's palm. "This leads under the temple. From there, we can get into the series of passages that will take us up to the extinct volcano. Once there, I can show you how to get to the Lake of Dreams."

"Sounds like a long way. Where's the cave?"

"I'll show you. Many have tried to find their way there on their own. Few make it."

"Wait!" Micah pulled back. The stench from the culvert oozed into his nostrils. He stifled a cough. "Why do you think I will make it?"

"The legends say you must believe enough in yourself to face your worst fears. If your sprit is weak, you will die. You tell the truth. You will survive."

Micah leaned against the rough stones, frowning in thought. Was this whole story just a Kudite myth? Or was there really a Cave of Truth? He remembered Attlad's father and how his visions influenced the campaigns. Real or not, the role of legend was apparently strong in this culture. Besides, what choice did he have?

"It will be getting light soon," Jaylun warned him, his fingers urgent on Micah's wrist. "We must begin the journey now."

Micah pulled himself up into the culvert and helped Jaylun replace the grate. He felt along the damp curved stone with his right hand. As he edged along after Jaylun, the stench became stronger and he pulled a part of the hood around to cover his nose. Rat-like creatures slithered over his boots.

For hours they moved steadily through the dank curving tunnels, only pausing to climb up a ladder and through to another level. Occasionally they would have to backtrack when Jaylun missed a turn or needed to check out one of the junctions with his small torch. Most of the time they moved in total darkness.

At last they saw daylight as they came around the final bend. Jaylun stopped abruptly.

"This is as far as I can take you today," he explained. "Wait here. You have food and drink. I will return as soon as I can."

"How long will that be? Hours? Days?"

"Chento, I will be missed if I disappear from my duties now. If that happens, Grir may be questioned. I cannot allow that. I will lead you to the edge of the lake tonight when I return. I will give you directions. After that, I can do no more."

"Good enough. See you then."

Micah watched Jaylun's slight figure as he rapidly disappeared around the bend in the tunnel. Then he took up his position as close to the outside as he dared. At least the air was cleaner there. He could breathe freely, even though he was still a wanted man.

Micah waited all day, sometimes dozing, sometimes watching the desolate landscape that stretched out on the other side of the bars. Well trained soldier that he was, he was careful not to eat too much of the food in his bag, knowing he might not be able to get more supplies. Every so often, he went through a series of stretching exercises to keep his muscles from seizing up. It was during one of these sessions that he realized his balls had returned to their normal size.

Jaylun was as good as his word. He came back that night and led Micah outside into the desolate landscape the young Kudite kept referring to as 'behind' the Citadel. It was a distinct relief for Micah to be outside again. Little by little he was regaining his old assurance, the skills of years of training and reconnaissance missions coming back to him as he skulked through the intermittent moonlight. There was no vegetation here on this high ground, and no sign of the Citadel except the dull bluish glow outlining the jagged peaks behind them. High in the rocks, he could see the faint gleam of candles now and then, but only if he looked carefully.

"That is from the temple," Jaylun explained. "No one else would have any opening from their home that might give access to anything from this side of the Citadel."

"Evil spirits?" Micah asked, only half serious.

Jaylun shrugged. "It is better not to know," he said simply. "Unless one wishes to study the Canon of our Ancestors, as I do," he added.

"Oh, I see." He didn't, but it was obviously another of those 'complicated' Kudite things that was difficult to understand.

They reached the Lake of Dreams a few hours later. It was an unpleasant surprise for Micah. The name had led him to expect a silver expanse, shaded by lacy trees, sort of like an oasis in the unrelenting gloom of the volcanic landscape. He stood on the shifting shale, staring down to where the water lay below them in a bowl of rock, black and slick and dangerous. There was no movement on its lifeless surface, no ripple of fish or insect. He shivered.

On the opposite shore loomed a vast cave, its mouth filled from side to side by the water.

"The Cave of Truth," Jaylun told him. "Inside, the floor of the cave is higher than the water, or so I am told."

"Is there a tide of some sort?" Micah asked, still puzzled.

"No. Nothing like that."

"How are you supposed to get there? Is there a boat?"

"No. You must swim. It is the only way to cleans the body. You are lucky, Chento. Sometimes the lake is much larger than it is now."

"Lucky?"

Jaylun nodded and waved his hand, already backing away towards the Citadel.

Micah suppressed an impatient sign, forcing his hands to silence. Swim. In this inky blackness. It was that, or return to certain death, he reminded himself. Slowly, he began to get out of his clothes.

TEN

he black water slid around his naked body like liquid ice. It took his breath away. For a moment, he stood perfectly still on the shelf of rock, gasping for air, waiting for his limbs to go numb. The water was up to his armpits. Frigid. Paralysing. His teeth began to chatter. He held up his bundle of clothes, wishing they could give him some protection against the unearthly chill of the water. When he turned his head, Jaylun was already a shadow, retreating into darker shadows.

Micah began to swim. It was awkward holding the bundle out of the water, but he had had practice doing this. It was only the terrible cold that gave him problems. It seemed to take forever for that life-giving tingle to work its way through his veins, letting him know he was alive after all. He swam slowly towards the looming darkness of the cave. His naked body barely caused a ripple in the inky water.

As he drew into the shadow of the cave, he thought about how he was trusting his life to Jaylun, this young alien male he had only met two nights ago, the lover of the man whose sole purpose in helping him was to gain status for himself. And yet, he had little choice. At least dying here would be more worthy of a soldier, he thought wryly. He would die trying to save another man's honour. That was a worthy goal.

His foot scraped against rock and he realized he was inside the mouth of the cave. Just as Jaylun had promised, the ground rose abruptly, so that he was on dry land a few feet inside the entrance. He was shivering so much it was difficult to get his clothes back on, but finally he was ready to explore. The small torch cast just enough light to throw wavering shadows high on the uneven rock-face as Micah started his journey deeper into the cave.

He didn't know what, exactly, he was expecting, but it certainly was not a tall man with long hair. It was hard to tell in the dim light what age he was, but something about him spoke of experience and ancient wisdom. He held a long staff with a pale green light glowing at the top end.

"I am Micah Starion," he began. "I am a Terran, come to ask your help." He held his hands in as much light as there was available, hoping the man could read the signs. It would be difficult enough explaining things.

"What are you hiding from us?"

Micah couldn't tell exactly how he knew what the man had said, but the message was clear enough. "Nothing," Micah answered. "Explain what you mean."

"No one comes to the Cave of Truth, hiding his body, and hiding his trust by bringing provisions."

Micah dropped his bag at once. There wasn't much left, anyway. "Forgive me if I do not know the customs here, sir. The clothes are for warmth, not to conceal."

The man didn't reply, but Micah could tell he was not impressed with this reasoning. The longer Micah stood there, facing the silent figure, yet unable to make out his features with any clarity, the more Micah felt the weight of that disapproval. Then the feeling changed. It was almost disappointment, verging towards disgust, that Micah felt in the air around him. Not just from one man, but from a group. There were more than just the two of them in the Cave, he realized. With that discovery, came fear. Not the straightforward fear of death in battle, but the more complex bone jarring dread that comes when we know there is something out there that is beyond our experience.

He began to get out of the clothes, his skin breaking out in gooseflesh as the chill hit his nakedness. Beneath his fear was anger that he was being reduced once again to the status of slave. Without even the hair on his head to cover him. As his pants dropped to the ground, he was aware of an odd current of air swirling around his feet, as if a door had been opened, letting in a draft. He shivered, lifting his feet free of the clothes. Then, it was if the clothes simply disappeared. Startled, he looked down, but could barely make out his own feet in the dimness, let alone anything else. Moving his right foot experimentally, he met no resistance. It was as if there had never been anything there.

He cleared his throat. "I am ready for any tests you may wish to give me," he said, signing as well, though he had the strong feeling communication here had no need of words.

"Why are you here?"

This question was a surprise. He had somehow assumed that these dwellers in the Cave of Truth were all-knowing. Or perhaps it was that they wanted him to express his purpose. He wrapped his arms around himself, trying to still the shivering that shook his body. His skin felt clammy and his own touch did little to warm him. He raised his head, feeling the damp air clinging to his shaved scalp, and began to tell the story of Attlad's unjust arrest for a murder that he had committed to save his ex master. "I gather that the only way I can testify for him and stand any chance of being believed, is if I pass through your Cave of Truth," he finished.

"What do you expect us to do for you?" The question hovered in the air before him.

Micah drew in his breath and squared his shoulders. "I'm not sure," he said. "I don't really understand it, but it's something to do with testing my integrity." He paused, looking for the right word. He had a sudden vivid memory of Attlad's father and the awe with which his visions and dreams were reported and studied. "I give you my dreams as evidence of my good faith," he said.

"Your soul."

"I will show you my soul, yes," he said cautiously, "in my dreams." For the first time, he sensed approval from the unseen men around him. Suddenly, he was no longer freezing.

"Your dreams are the dreams of a warrior — and a sex slave, since you are both."

"I do not come here as a slave," Micah protested. Unconsciously he threw back his broad shoulders and raised his head challengingly.

"But you are both. There is no shame in being a sexual warrior."

The term sounded odd to Micah, but if that was how they looked at things, it was fine by him. Now that he thought of it, it was a very apt term to describe his life with Attlad, a life that seemed very far away at the moment.

In front of him, the tall shadowy figure moved deeper into the cave. His pale hand beckoned Micah to follow. This time, there seemed to be no need of a torch. His bare feet walked unerringly over the smooth beaten earth floor, as long as he kept his eyes on the moving shadow in front of him. Once, he turned his head, trying to get a clearer idea of his surroundings. Instantly, he stumbled. Around him, he felt that surge of disapproval again, as if he had failed some sort of test he wasn't even aware of. The feeling of being watched, returned. His cock stiffened slightly.

The ground had been rising steadily, along with the temperature. His navigator's mind knew they were now well above the level of the cave opening. The floor under his feet no longer felt like pounded earth, but was more like smooth marble. Ahead of him, a pale light reflected off the gleaming wall. They were coming to some sort of a chamber. The path veered to the right. Turning the corner, he stopped in surprise.

Before him was a vast chamber filled with a green glow. The light glistened along slender icicles of crystal, thick as a man's arm, that hung from the vaulted ceiling almost to the glass-smooth floor. The walls were pebbled with mirror-like bits of black, that refracted the light back in tiny jewelled shards that dazzled his eyes, making him unsure of what he was really seeing. He had a fleeting impression of a group of tall male figures around the edges of the space, but when he looked closer, the image vanished, replaced by the green lights, dancing with the shadows. When he looked back to his guide, he saw a young man, standing before him in a ray of light. His long robe was open and he was naked underneath. Micah was not really surprised to see that his guide was not the old white-haired man he had thought him to be.

"Stand over there." The man's voice was deep, filling the great space, yet quiet and firm.

Micah walked to the area between two giant icicles, and stood on a sort of platform.

"Now, tell us, in your own words, why you have made this journey."

Micah began to talk, slowly at first, unsure whether or

not he was being understood. When it became clear that they knew what he was saying, he was soon caught up in his own tale, trying to lay it all out before them in as clear an unbiased a way as possible. When he finished, there was a long silence.

"We understand what you have told us," the guide said. "We hear the words of the warrior. Now, show us your soul. Take hold of the crystal pillars, stretching as high as you can on either side."

Micah did as he was told, aware that many unseen eyes were devouring his naked body. He found pleasure in the warmth of their gaze. He stood easily between the columns, legs apart, as he had been taught. As he reached high above his head and touched the rough surface of the stalactites, he was startled to find he could no longer move his hands. He was held as captive as if he were shackled in chains to the pillars. When he tried to shift his feet, he found it impossible.

"Is this your idea of a sexual warrior?" he cried, pulling against his invisible bonds. No amount of writhing could loosen them, however. He was securely imprisoned, hanging on display, bathed in the unearthly green light.

He felt, rather than saw, the others gather around him, felt the touch of male hands on his body. Cool fingers grazed against his skin, lingering on the welts and scars left by Kerdas's whip, and as each one was touched, it flamed alive and pain jolted through him anew. He clenched his teeth, holding the hurt inside, willing it through his body. Each re-opened wound brought with it the memory of how and when it was inflicted, and he relived the intense experience again, and again. As the hands moved over him, Micah screamed and cried out and cursed, as the lash bit through his skin anew, until his throat was raw, his muscles strained and aching and his mind afire with agony.

And then a hand touched his cock. His eyes sprang

open and he looked into the jet black eyes of his guide, and he saw there the image of Attlad, holding him in his arms while his master's symbol, the red dragon, was tattooed on his cock. At once he felt a shock of pleasure so intense, he thought he would come. He looked down to see his cock jutting out from his naked crotch, the dragon proud and rampant.

"Attlad," said his guide, and the others murmured around him. Assent? But what did it mean?

Micah was now totally confused, as the men withdrew their touch, leaving him without feeling, his cock aching, his asshole throbbing, sucking at the empty air. He felt tears in his eyes for the first time. All the pain was as nothing to this desolation. His chest heaved as the longing surged through him.

Then, without warning, he was free. He staggered, supporting himself against the pillar with one hand. For the first time he saw the other men, walking away from him in single file, a long line of men, naked except for a bright chain looped over one shoulder and crossing to hang against the opposite hip like a bandolier. The metal links caught the light and glittered, the brilliance hurting his eyes. When the last man had reached the centre of the room, his guide joined the line. As if on a signal, Micah fell into step behind him.

As the file progressed through the cavern, a swell of sound rose up around them. It was faint, at first, like the breaking of waves upon a distant shore; then grew louder as the long column wound its way through the maze of crystal stalactites and into another chamber, beyond.

Micah moved to the centre of the area and walked up the short flight of steps there. The others formed a circle around him. Once again he was bathed in the strange green light, shining down on him like a spotlight from directly above. Without being told, he again placed his hands on the stalactites on either side of his small platform and stood immobile, his feet apart, firmly attached by the unseen bonds.

Then the circle wavered and broke. As the strange sounds swirled around them, one man approached Micah and stood in front of him, his mouth on a level with the Terran's still engorged cock. Closing his eyes, he took Micah's cock into his mouth in one smooth motion, sucking it down his throat. Micah threw back his head and moaned. The wonderful sensations purred around his eager cock, the throat muscles working it skilfully until he came in a burst of pent-up passion. The music crashed around him. At once, the man opened his eyes, slid the deflating cock out of his mouth and rejoined the circle.

Immediately, the next man took his place and repeated the process. Micah shook and moaned with pleasure as yet again, he came. When the third man took the wilting meat in his mouth, Micah protested, but to no avail. There was no way to stop the process, which was fast becoming an insidious torture as his nuts were sucked dry again. And again. And again. It took longer and longer, but somehow, each man brought him to shuddering orgasm, until even the thought of his cock getting hard, made him whimper. It was then that the guide approached him.

"No!" cried Micah. "Oh God, not again!"

The man in front of him raised his hand in an imperious gesture. His face now seemed ageless, his pale skin taut over well-toned muscles. Micah felt his protest die in his throat. The odd swell of sound retreated. In the silence, the sudden movement of the men in the circle unnerved him. There was a crash, followed by a juddering clatter as gold chains slid off broad shoulders, the links clinking together. Micah shuddered, the noise set his teeth on edge. Goose bumps brook out on his skin. As if at a signal, the men took the chains in their right hands and swung them towards their neighbour. As the left hands caught the bright links, a true circle formed joining the men and the chains. In some way Micah didn't understand, the atmosphere thickened, as if all the energy of the place were gathered right here in the circle around him.

Once again his invisible bonds released him. The air condensed around him, pressing against him, lifting him up, up, until he was immersed in the soft green light, suspended above the circle, his arms and legs still spread wide. He looked down and saw the guide, his right arm held high. His palm began to move backwards, as if he were balancing a tray above his head. Slowly Micah's body tilted until he lay as if on a board in the middle of the cave. Gradually he descended until he felt the cool hard pressure of smooth stone against his back. He realized he had been holding his breath. He began to pant, short, hard puffs of air that rasped in his throat. His heart knocked in his chest. His body dripped with sweat. They were playing tricks with his mind, he told himself. That's all it was. Mind games, like they used to do with young cadets at the Academy, like Attlad did to him back at the complex. But reason could not hold on to what was happening here. Reason itself slid away as he fought to get his breath, to move his hands down from above his head. Who were these people?

The low wail of the eerie music started up again as the guide came into his line of vision. Now he was carrying something in front of him on a tray, but Micah couldn't make out what it was. The light gleamed on the man's muscular body, bringing out the lines of his biceps, his pectorals. His cock was thick, half hard in its nest of coarse black hair. Micah licked his lips and looked up at the man's impassive face.

THE CITADEL

Candles. They were small votive candles on the tray and the leader, as Micah now thought of him, began to place them on Micah's prone body. Everywhere the small cylinders of wax touched his skin he felt a tiny shock. This at least was something he understood. His breathing evened out. His muscles jumped in anticipation. He clenched and unclenched his fists.

The leader slid the tray out of sight underneath the stone table. He leaned over Micah, his black eyes glittering, refracting the green light as if they were jewels. Suddenly, the candles were lit, how he didn't understand. The tiny flames danced over the Terran's helpless body and he watched as the wax began to melt, pooling next to the burning wicks, ready to spill over onto his naked flesh if he moved. He swallowed hard. Little sparks of sexual tension danced just under his skin, making his tits stand out. His cock began to stiffen. No! Micah tried to will it back to its flaccid state. He had had too much. The pain of his erection would shake through his body, leaving splashes of melted wax to burn new scars against his flesh.

Control. Breathe carefully. Keep it shallow so no breath would move his chest, holding the candles perfectly still. Micah watched each tiny flame, mesmerised as the melting pools grew deeper, larger, until finally the inevitable happened. Scalding wax slid over onto his body. Small jolts of pain seared his belly, his left groin, his right nipple. He clenched his jaw, determined to keep in control. He had taken much more severe assaults on his body than this.

From the corner of his eye, he saw the leader slide the heavy gold chain off his shoulder. The metal seemed to slither down his arm. The Kudite moved to the foot of the table and stood there, arms outstretched, the gleaming chain held with both great hands. Micah stared at him through the golden haze of the candles, his vision blurred by pain. Although his head was not restrained in any way, he couldn't look away, rivetted by the tall imposing figure who now slid the gold links of the chain onto the slab of rock. The metal bent into a sinuous glittering line, than separated with a soft hiss. Micah felt the scream rise in his throat as the golden snakes reared up for a moment and then slithered between his legs. His body spasmed with fear, sending rivulets of liquid pain spilling across his chest, his belly, his shaved groin. A low moan escaped from his throat, rising higher in short gasps as the creatures undulated up onto his thighs. There were three or four of them, their dry scaly bodies sending odd shivers across the surface of Micah's skin as they reared up and looked about, their thin red tongues darting in and out as if in search of prey. Their jewel-like eyes glittered.

Another gasp sent more wax searing onto his skin. His cock was hard. Attlad's red dragon stood up tall and proud and the snakes turned slowly, their cold stares watching intently. The closest one struck first. Its teeth, razor sharp, sent needle-like stabs into his cock. Micah began to struggle at last. Terror and pain overcame all rational thought. His screams cut through the air as the wax slid over his skin, coating his body in heat. The snakes reacted with a concerted attack on his cock, that was now rock hard. Then one snake wrapped its scaly body around his penis. Arching his back, Micah's scream turned into a long wail of ecstasy as he came in great arcing spurts, over and over and over again. He wouldn't have thought it possible, after what he had been through, but the long strings of creamy liquid were proof enough that this was real. When it was over, he collapsed back on the rock, spent. As his eyes refocused, he saw the snakes loop around each other as they slid off his crotch and reformed into a chain. He closed his eyes.

The rock beneath him shuddered and began to move.

His eyes sprang open in terror as the stone slab he was fastened to with invisible bonds, rose towards the vaulted ceiling of the cave, gathering speed as it went. The air rushed past his ears. Green light exploded in brightness, almost blinding him. And then, with a great crash, everything went black.

ELEVEN

icah shivered convulsively and opened his eyes. Rain poured down in sheets. Forked lightening split the sky. Thunder crashed around him. Micah sat up, surprised to find he was free, and hugged himself. The cave had vanished, replaced with towering mountain peaks that gleamed jagged and unearthly in the blue glow of lightning.

Then he realized with a shock that we was dry! All this water pouring down, cascading in rivers over the slippery black rocks, and yet, he was untouched by the storm that raged around him. He took a deep breath and stepped off the rock table. At once, rain almost blinded him. There was something cleansing about the cold reality of the water, and he stood, legs apart, head back, and took the full violence of it against his nakedness. Whatever weirdness he had just been through, this, at least, was real! He scraped off the wax that coated his chest and belly.

It was the cold that finally brought him to his senses; that and his instinct for survival that had been honed through years of training that had finally led to the title of

Nebula Warrior. He wanted to refuse the beckoning haven offered by the stone slab, not trusting the mystical powers of the strange Kudite phenomenon, but there was no shelter anywhere else. Cautiously he climbed back up on the stone table. The rock felt warm against his ass and thighs as he sat cross-legged, staring at the storm around him. The eerie calm of this magic capsule was unsettling, but he tried to close his eyes to the mystery and concentrate instead on how he was to get out of here.

In a few minutes, he was dry and his body had stopped shaking. The storm seemed to be tapering off, the thunder rumbling in the distance, fading away as the rain slowed to a gentle patter. Micah had still reached no conclusions about how he was to get back to some semblance of civilization. There were no stars visible to help him figure out the direction of the Citadel, no vegetation that would give him a chance to dig a burrow for shelter. He was wondering about some way to extend the protection of this magical rock, when he became aware of a presence moving towards him in the dimness. He crouched, ready to defend himself.

"You are safe, now," a voice said. He heard it in his head rather than in the air, but it was clear, low, reassuring. Familiar.

"Who are you?" Micah asked, although he was sure he knew the answer. The figure was close enough for him to make out the gleam of black eyes, the pale skin glowing with an inner light, and it was possible to make out his strong features — the wide flaring eyebrows, that beak of a nose, and that long mouth that could be so cruel one minute and then quirk into a smile the next.

"I am your guide in this voyage to the truth," the voice intoned.

"I've been telling the truth all along," Micah said. "Do you believe me now?"

"Before, your truth was invisible, as you were. Now, we have imbibed your very essence, have tasted your body, your soul and your mind. We have felt what you have felt, seen what you have seen. Nothing was hidden from us. Now others will hear and believe, because of our testimony."

Micah turned away, vaguely embarrassed. He should feel insulted that his word alone meant nothing to these people. They knew who he was, who he had been before coming here, of his own free will. Free will. Perhaps that was the problem. Whether or not the choice had been his made no difference to these people. He thought of Grir, a man who had sacrificed a great deal to make himself a respected warrior in his country, but here, that choice was not acknowledged. Grir could never achieve again the respect this choice entitled him to at home.

Micah turned back to his guide. The man looked older, now. Still strong and vibrant, his black hair was now streaked with grey, his face weathered and lined.

"Who are you, really?" Micah asked again.

"That is the wrong question."

Micah looked down at his own nakedness and frowned in concentration. "Where is the proof that I have actually been here?"

The man smiled approvingly. He stepped closer and produced a pale green stone on a thong and hung it around Micah's neck. "This is a key that will open many doors. And here is a message string that will release Attlad into your hands." He laid a pattern of coloured knotted silk strands on the rock beside him. "You will find that things have been restored to the way they were before the attack on your former master. And we have summoned Kerdas before our High Council."

"He will be punished?"

"He will answer to us for what he has done. Now you

must go. You will be led to the place where Attlad is. The door will open to you. After that, what you decide is up to you."

"Attlad is free to go?"

"Once you get there, yes."

It seemed far too simple. After what he had been through, it was almost ludicrous. Micah ran a hand over his shaved head, thinking. He was surprised to feel a soft fuzz of new growth. "How long have I been here?" he asked suddenly.

The guide ignored the question. He reached inside his robe and withdrew a wineskin. "Drink. You must be thirsty."

Micah took the wineskin gratefully and put it to his lips. His throat was dry in spite of the rainwater he had gulped. He tilted his head back as the sweet fruity liquid slid down his parched throat. He closed his eyes, feeling a strange comforting warmth spread through him. When he heard the warning bells in his mind, it was too late.

When Micah opened his eyes again, he was in the ruined courtyard beside the old temple. Far above him, the sun shone down illuminating the ancient walls and dusty windows, the vines that twisted along the rotting balcony railings and the moss growing along one side of the courtyard. Was it real, he wondered, or merely a recreation of sunlight?

He looked at himself and found he was dressed in a shirt and leather pants. On top of that was a loose cloak with a hood, all far better than what he had had before. Highly polished boots were on his feet. Around his neck, the green stone glowed as if reflecting the pale sunlight. It was the only proof that all this hadn't just been a dream.

"Shit," muttered Micah, getting to his feet. He felt stiff,

his joints protesting, as if he had been in one position for a very long time. When he walked, his groin itched, reminding him that his body had not been shaved for some days. He felt his head and found that his hair, too, was growing back. How long had he been in the cave? His guide never had answered that question.

By trial and error, he made his way back to the one area of the Citadel that was most familiar to him from his walks with Grir. No one paid any attention to the tall hooded figure as he strode along, trying to give the impression that he knew exactly where he was going. Several times he had to retrace his steps, and at last, he paused, scanning the faces of the passers by, looking for a likely candidate who might help him. It would have to be a slave, he thought, someone who would expect hand signals. He had no idea how to locate the place where Attlad was held. Just one more detail the soothsayer had neglected to fill him in on. He had said merely that he would be taken there. By whom?

And then he saw the pearlboys. There were two of them, hurrying along together, shaved heads down, bare feet noiseless on the metal walkway. They wore identical short tunics of an almost sheer white. Their little asses were plainly visible as they started up a stairway in front of him.

Micah reached out and tugged at the short skirt of the nearest boy. As he paused, Micah's hand cupped the firm flesh of the boy's ass appreciatively.

"Lord?" The signs were slow and careful, as if the boy was uncertain how this obvious stranger would react to hand gestures.

"Where do I find the place where prisoners are kept?" Micah asked.

At once the boy's eyes filled with uncertainty. "Prisoners?" he asked.

The other boy stepped forward and said something to

his companion quickly. "I know who you are," he signed rapidly to Micah. "We cannot help you because our master will be angry if we are late. If you ask any guard and show what you wear around your neck, he will take you there." He grabbed his companion's hand and pulled him up the steps.

Micah watched them go, fingering the stone absently as he studied their sturdy legs, imagining the tiny cocks nestled in their silver and blue beads. He wondered how Bar was, and if he would ever see him again.

"Excuse me, sir." The young man in front of him was signing rapidly. His dark eyes looked excited. "Do you wish help?"

Micah repeated his question, careful to let the young man see the green stone clearly. Obviously the stone was the reason for this sudden friendly gesture.

The young man wore a uniform Micah didn't recognize, and after a few more questions, during which Micah mentioned Attlad's name, he agreed to lead the way to the principal jail.

After a walk of about ten minutes, they arrived at a small door with a grilled window beside it. The young man knocked and spoke rapidly to an unseen presence on the other side of the grill. He gestured to Micah, then to the green stone.

"You will have no trouble, lord," he said, turning back to Micah. "The gate-man will let you in and take you to the prisoner you seek." The young man didn't wait for any thanks, but hurried away into the crowd. Micah wondered if he had, in some subtle way, won more status for himself by recognizing the green stone and offering his help.

The gate keeper didn't seem eager to escort Micah anywhere. He slid the grill open and peered at him in silence for a full minute, before slamming the grate closed again.

The small door creaked open slowly, and as Micah stepped inside, lights snapped on, showing a wide bare corridor leading to a barred door. The old man led the way, muttering to himself about having to do everything around here these days and other things Micah didn't quite catch. He unlocked the bared door and went through. Micah followed.

Inside, the floor was a metal grate and down below, he saw the huddled figures of the prisoners. A noise above his head made he look up. Here was another grate, which served as floor to another tier of prisoners caged above them. Several bearded faces pressed against the metal bars, their naked bodies rolled into a tight ball as they crouched on their knees, peering down at them. The silence was eerie.

The keeper checked a row of names and numbers.

"Attlad," Micah reminded him, watching over his shoulder.

The old man nodded impatiently and selected a round disk from one of the hooks. He slid the disk into a slot by the light switch and pulled a lever. A groaning of gears ensued and slowly, one of the cages up above began to descend. With a bone-jarring thud, it stopped about ten feet from Micah.

The keeper stuck out his hand. He said something Micah couldn't grasp. When he repeated the word, annoyed at the alien's slowness. Micah suddenly remembered the knotted message string and handed that over. Apparently satisfied, the old man rummaged in a locker, hauled out a large cloth bag and threw it at Micah's feet. Then he handed him the red disk. "You have fifteen minutes. After that, the doors will lock." He turned and shuffled off.

Micah approached the cage and slid back the door. Attlad stood with his back to him, legs apart, hands holding onto the bars to steady himself. His bare back and muscular thighs were streaked with welts from the whip. The hairy ass Micah knew so well had been shaved. He was obviously expecting some sort of punishment.

"Attlad," Micah whispered.

The man slowly turned. For a brief moment, the slate grey eyes swept over Micah, then, locked onto his face. The expression was one of astonishment, confusion. Anger? Micah was at a loss as to what to do next. He hadn't once stopped to think how Attlad would feel about this sudden reversal of their roles — how he would handle it. He waited, forcing himself to let Attlad make the next move. He noted the silver collar around the man's neck. It had a round disk-shaped box that pressed into the hollow of his throat.

To Micah's amazement, Attlad dropped his eyes and went down on his knees before his former slave. A strange thrill went through the Terran man, seeing his master like this, naked and vulnerable before him, but the voice of reason put a stop to any fantasising. They had to get out of here. Later on there would be time to figure out their relationship.

Without a word, Micah handed the bag of clothing to Attlad, but the Kudite made no move to take out the clothes. Instead, he raised his head and touched the collar around his neck. The grey eyes burned with an emotion Micah couldn't quite place. There was pain, but also anger, humiliation. And something else….

As Micah looked more closely at the collar, he saw the disk was thicker than he had realized. There was a ridge around the outside, the same size. The size of the red disk the keeper had given him. Bending forward, he fitted the large coin into the slot and heard a distinct click. To his surprise, the collar stayed in place, but the round box came away in his hand, leaving an open sore on the skin of

Attlad's throat.

"So that's why everyone's so silent here," Micah said.

"It is better than cutting out our tongues," whispered Attlad. It had obviously been a while since he had used his voice.

Micah stepped outside the cage while Attlad dressed, trying not to see the anguished faces around him. Now that he understood this eerie silence, he couldn't bare to look at the prisoners. When Attlad was dressed, Micah led the way back to the small door. Micah pounded on the grill on the wall to get the old man's attention. After making them wait a few minutes, the keeper finally pulled the lever that opened the door, and they walked out into the morning crowds.

"They promised me that everything would be restored the way it was before the attack on you," Micah told Attlad. "I assume that means you still have your living quarters. Let's go there."

Attlad stared at him for a moment, then turned away and began to walk quickly through the crowd. As Micah followed, his uneasiness grew. It was more than just the Kudite's silence. That he could understand. There was something more. Something was drastically wrong.

Attlad's apartments surprised Micah with their elegant simplicity. Here, there was none of the silken opulence evident in Dadani's residence, or the languid luxury of the pearlboys' Quarters; none of the heavy ugly ironwork he had seen in the public areas. These rooms were large and high-ceilinged, with little furniture except what was needed: several leather sling chairs, a table, a trunk in one corner. The stark white walls were unadorned, except for the astounding display of weapons that filled one wall, floor to ceiling. In the middle was a shield, painted with the red dragon rampant that was Attlad's personal symbol. The sight of it reminded Micah of the tattoo on his cock. He blushed and turned back to the study of the swords and hand polished spears, the arrows and bows and slings of varying sizes. They were all hand to hand combat weapons and Micah had seen them used in demonstrations of expertise often at the Complex. Much of the Kudite battle code, he had learned, had to do with contests between warriors sent out to fight on behalf of their troop, though Micah had never figured out how this worked in practice.

The other thing that struck him at once about the place was the unusual amount of daylight pouring in at the windows. Attlad must have a high status to be awarded rooms on the outer areas of the Citadel. He remembered the lack of sunlight in Grir's quarters as contrasted with Dadani's gardens and realized how much importance the status of warrior brought with it.

Through an open doorway, he saw a large bed, the four posts at each corner going right to the ceiling. The bed itself appeared to be in the middle of the room, and along the far wall was a huge armoire. The other door led into a smaller room with a table and boxes piled against one wall.

Micah could feel the tension in the room crackle like static against his nerves. For the first time, the thought came to him that his relationship with Attlad was over. Perhaps that accounted for this feeling of uneasiness. Attlad himself had killed it when he gave him away, for whatever reason. It had been foolish, that dream that this, too, could be put back the way it used to be, just because he had made the journey through the Cave of Truth. But even as these thoughts coursed through his mind, he felt hot rebellion against this man he had gone through so much to be with. He swung around, words boiling up inside.

Attlad stood in the middle of the room, with nothing on but the dull metal collar from the prison. Micah stared in shock.

"What does this mean?" he said, articulating the alien words carefully.

Attlad raised his head, surprise in the cool grey eyes. Micah realized the Kudite had probably never heard his voice before, certainly not speaking his own language.

"I see you have learned a great deal," Attlad said. "You must know, then, that for my sins, you are now my master. I am sure you are very pleased to have me finally in your power."

Micah threw himself into one of the chairs with a Terran curse. "Why would I want this? I want only to free you from a false charge of murder. That is all, can you understand that? I see there is no such thing as gratefulness on the part of a Kudite lord!"

"Why would I be grateful?" cried Attlad, his voice hoarse. "I am ruined! I have no honour left to my name, thanks to what you have done! Why did you come back?"

"To save your miserable life, ingrate!"

"I would rather die with honour, than live as your slave!"

Micah laughed. When he looked at Attlad, he saw the man was trembling with rage. But he made himself stand there, naked, legs apart as he had trained Micah to do, his hands locked behind his back. The laughter died away in Micah's throat as admiration took over. Even unkempt and unshaved, Attlad was beautiful, his strong stocky body muscular and utterly desirable. Micah let his hot blue gaze take in every inch of the Kudite's body; the broad shoulders, the dark hairy chest, the heavy pecs, the hard belly, those solid thighs and in between them, that huge cock that made his throat ache with longing. It was half hard, he noticed and smiled. Obviously, seeing Micah again was not totally unpleasant!

"Turn around," Micah signed, returning to the language used with slaves to make it even worse for Attlad. If this was what he expected, let him have it.

Swallowing hard, Attlad hesitated just enough to show his hostility, then gave one final glare and turned around. They had shaved his ass in prison, and there were scars on his back and buttocks from the beatings he had taken. Micah felt a strange perverse thrill, seeing the welts. He got up and ran his hands over the man's hot flesh, his finger tips lingering on the raised scars. He felt the muscles jump and twitch under his touch.

Moving lower, his hands parted the smooth cheeks and he saw that the crack had been shaved too. The brown wrinkled eye of the asshole stood out clearly, defenceless and exposed. Micah trailed one finger down that dark road and slid the fingertip inside, up to the first knuckle.

Attlad caught his breath and trembled. It must be very hard to hold onto his control, Micah thought. Had anyone dared to do this to the warrior Attlad before? He felt the man's sphincter contract around his finger, sucking at him even as the man tried to deny his need.

"Relax," Micah murmured, and dropped his lips to the tender nape of the man's neck. He tasted salt and sweat and that wonderful harsh musk of the man he had lusted after for so long. He opened his mouth and sucked at the soft flesh, watching it turn bright red, dripping with his own saliva. He shoved a second finger inside his tight hole. This time, Attlad's clasped hands moved to push him away. Micah slapped his ass hard, his hand raising a red blush instantly. Attlad growled low in his throat.

"If you are now my slave, you will act like a slave," Micah snarled, the resistance banishing all tenderness he had felt just a moment ago. "Bend over and hold your ankles. Now!" He pushed down on Attlad's neck sharply. Meeting the expected resistance, he struck the other ass cheek hard, bringing a matching redness there.

"How dare you!" growled Attlad, turning to face him.

Micah smiled. "I have dared a lot more than this. Or have you forgotten already how you come to be here, rather than in that animal's cage you call a prison? Now, obey, or suffer the penalty."

Attlad spat at his feet. "What penalty? Your displeasure?"

"In the circumstances, my displeasure should mean a lot to you. Unless, that is, you are not the man of honour you pretend to be." He stared into the stormy grey eyes, and for the first time saw raw emotion there. Fury. Helplessness. Attlad hated the situation but there was nothing he could do about it. "On your knees and lick up the floor you have just defiled. Then I will fuck you."

Attlad started to speak, then changed his mind and clamped his mouth shut so hard his lip bled. But he sank to his knees and did as Micah had commanded, his tongue licking up all trace of his own spittle. Then he stood up, bent over and grasped his ankles.

Micah slid off his belt as he studied that muscular ass, so much paler than the rest of Attlad's hard soldier's body. The hand prints were already fading from the exposed, shaved skin. The asshole was clearly visible, its puckered lips shining with mucous. His balls hung low, still covered with their coat of dark fur, and his cock swung free, still half engorged, the head a deep luscious purple. Micah licked his lips and slid his belt out of his pants.

He heard the sharp intake of breath as Attlad saw what he was about to do. His face turned an angry red. But he didn't flinch as the leather cracked against his ass, gritting his teeth and taking the pain like the soldier he was. Micah drew back his arm and threw his whole weight behind the next blow, and the next, and the one after that. Still Attlad took it, his face contorted with pain and the determination not to give in.

Micah paused and opened his shirt. He was hot, the anger and lust coursing through him like electricity. So this was what it was like! But something reminded him that Attlad the master was driven by control, not the fury that lashed him on now. This was not being a master. This was revenge. He drew back his arm and struck Attlad again. By now, the Kudite's body was aflame with red stripes. Sweat poured down his face and back and thighs, glistening on the smooth reddened skin, matting the thick hair on his legs and chest and arms. He took the beating well, but his body was beginning to betray him. His cock was harder now, and tears squeezed out of his angry eyes. He was trembling, too, and it was harder to keep his balance. Micah smiled with satisfaction and brought the belt down on the inside of his thigh. Attlad yelped as the end curled against his balls.

Micah laughed. As he raised the belt again, he paused. "What is that noise?"

Attlad had trouble speaking, but at last he said. "There is someone at the door." He began to straighten up.

"Stay where you are," Micah said, putting his jacket back on.

"No! You cannot do this—"

"I can, and I will. Be silent." Micah went to the heavy wooden door and opened it. "Dadani!"

TWELVE

icah was suddenly very conscious of the belt he carried in his hand. He knew the woman could see Attlad behind him in the room, his naked ass sticking up in the air. "We were not expecting visitors," he said carefully, watching the surprise in her beautiful face as he spoke the Kudite words. "If you will wait a moment?" He bowed and closed the door, leaving her outside.

Attlad must have known he was plainly visible to anyone at the door, but much to Micah's delight, he had not moved. Micah went back beside him and picked up a smooth sphere from a copper bowl on the table. It was about two inches in diameter and had Kudite symbols of some sort carved into it. In spite of the symbols, however, the thing was smooth as glass. Micah spat on the ball, placed it against Attlad's asshole and pushed it slowly and steadily up inside the Kudite.

"Something to remind you of your new status, even as you play the host," Micah said, giving the ball a final shove as it disappeared inside Attlad's ass. "Get dressed. I'll let the lady in." Without a word, Attlad scooped up his clothes and went carefully out of the room.

Micah felt a strange elation as he went to the door. He enjoyed watching the confusion she tried to hide as he ushered her to a chair and sat down opposite her, like a host prepared to entertain his visitor. It was obvious that she felt awkward at this sudden change in roles. It was equally obvious that she didn't know what to call him. She solved the problem by not addressing him by name.

"News of your testimony on behalf of Attlad at the Cave of Truth arrived at the Council this morning," she said slowly, making sure he understood her words. Almost as if she's speaking to a child, Micah thought annoyed. He nodded, to show he was following. "I want to welcome you to this new stage of your life. Congratulations."

He nodded graciously. He did not intend to make it easier for her.

Attlad arrived at that point, dressed as Micah was in leather pants and a simple white shirt. He had brushed his dark hair and washed his face and looked almost his usual self, except that his dull metal collar was plainly visible.

"Welcome to my home, Dadani," he said, and kissed her fingertips.

"Welcome back, Attlad," she replied. "I bring you these." She opened the bag she carried and withdrew two balls, similar to the one Attlad now carried up his ass, except these were larger and of a more valuable metal. Micah glanced at Attlad and saw him blush, and he smiled. She handed the larger one to Attlad, the smaller one to Micah.

Attlad turned to Micah, his grey eyes bright with suppressed laughter. "These are apology spheres," he explained. "The carving tells about the offence that is regretted. The one that used to be on that table was from my brother

Kerdas, presented many years ago." His eyes locked into Micah's holding them a moment longer.

"I see," said Micah, grinning. "That one is where it belongs, then."

"Apparently," Attlad agreed, his mouth twitching slightly in amusement.

Dadani looked puzzled. "I owe you both more than can be put onto the surface of a sphere," she said. "I have allowed myself to be unduly influenced by a man who hates you, Attlad. I knew that at the time, but somehow, I lost sight of this fact as time went by. You were so far away…and he was always here…."

"I understand," Attlad said. "Kerdas can be very persuasive. You forget that I have seen him at work many times. Even our parents believed him, most of the time." His face was grim, now, as he thought back over the years.

"It is a good thing you have someone who does believe you. Always." She smiled at Micah, and although that was not true, he let it go. He turned the sphere around and around in his hands as he listened to them talk.

"Kerdas has been arrested for setting up the attempt on your life, Attlad. He is also held responsible for the death of the guard in his employ," she went on, glancing at Micah. "You are a dangerous man," she added, smiling. "I had no idea of the value of the gift Attlad sent me until it was too late."

"But you asked for Chento," Attlad said. "Surely you knew—Was that Kerdas's idea too?"

"Yes. He insisted it would prove the sincerity of your intentions if I asked for something you really cared about as a bond gift. I think he was actually surprised when Chento arrived."

"So was I," remarked Micah softly.

"Kerdas always has wanted whatever I value," Attlad

said, his voice tight. "Always!"

"I knew he was trying to get back at you through me," Micah said, resorting to signals now that the conversation was getting more complex. "Nothing else could explain his cruelty."

"He is a sadist," Attlad signed. For a moment he laid a hand on Micah's hand, and they both forgot the roles they had been playing. Micah had a sudden urge to throw himself on the floor between Attlad's knees and lay his head against his great muscular thigh. He caught himself in time and turned back to Dadani, who was speaking.

"Excuse me, I don't understand?" Micah said after a moment. Attlad was looking surprised and pleased about something. He was actually preening.

"I am renewing the offer of marriage," Dadani explained. "When Attlad was arrested, naturally the marriage plans were cancelled. Now that everything is set right again, I see no reason not to go through with the ceremony. I still wish to be allied with a warrior, especially one who's father is a Truth Dreamer."

"And I still wish to be allied with you, Dadani. You are a valued Council member and held in high esteem by the people of the Citadel."

Micah felt a chill spreading inside. He didn't understand what was happening. All he knew was that for the first time, he felt jealousy that someone else might be chosen by this man. Why did Attlad want to get married? What was it Grir had said? Something about owning property?

As if reading his mind, Attlad turned to address him. "Micah," he said, startling Micah so much his mouth dropped open. "You must understand what marriage means here. I will still be free to return to the outposts and fight on the front lines, but I can now become a warlord, a leader of more than just a small group of men. You will still—" He paused. "Perhaps I presume too much."

"I have yet to decide my future plans," Micah said stiffly. He felt as if his lips were frozen, it was so hard to speak. "This is something for us to discuss privately."

"So you agree the ceremony will go on, Attlad?" Dadani said.

"I agree," Attlad replied. "Will it be the same time as we planned before?"

"Everything will be the same, except—" She looked doubtfully at Micah, then back to Attlad. "Except for the entertainment."

"That is up to Micah."

"There is a lot of money riding on this match," Dadani went on. Although Micah knew the words were meant for him, she still addressed Attlad. "I know Grir's master will want him to participate."

Micah thought of that muscled dark body with the greenish sheen. He felt he owed a debt to Grir for getting him out of the Quarters. But just as he was about to agree to the match, he remembered the needle feeding in steroids and hormones and who knew what else to keep the alien fighter mean and fit, to give him an advantage. This man had not lost a fight for a long time. The stakes would be very high for him. He would *have* to win. They were both waiting for him to reply. Dadani looked annoyed at his hesitation. Attlad's expression was unreadable.

"I'm sure you can find another candidate worthy to fight Grir," he said.

Dadani bit back her reply. She gathered up her bag, obviously angry. "I must go. I left the council meeting to come here, Attlad. I will see you in a few days at the ceremony."

She got to her feet, bowed regally to Attlad and merely nodded to Micah. Attlad glanced at him before following her to the door. As she looked at him one last time before leaving, he kissed the metal sphere. She gave him a tight smile and walked away.

Attlad came back and laid the sphere on the table. He looked at Micah, his grey eyes dark with a look that stirred the Terran's pulse. "Why will you not fight at my wedding?" he asked.

"Because I am not your slave, Attlad. Because I have nothing to prove. I always knew the fight on board the ship was not fair. Now I know this one would not be fair, either."

"I hear you have been training. This time, you would be prepared."

"The only fair fight would be a match between Grir and another eunuch who uses the needle to compensate for what he has. had removed."

Attlad nodded thoughtfully. "I must explain something to you. I had to make it look that I had a reason to want to give you up," he said. "I would lose face with my men if I gave away my prized P.B. as a bond gift. Kerdas knew that, though I don't think Dadani does."

Micah said nothing. All he saw was that he had been through hell so that Attlad would not lose face.

"Are you going to leave me?" Attlad asked suddenly.

"I have been thinking about going back to my own people," Micah said.

The two men stood facing each other for a moment longer. Then, Attlad began to undress, his eyes never leaving Micah's face as the clothes dropped to the floor at his feet. Micah watched that beautiful nakedness slowly appear, the skin still red, marked by his belt. He felt the heat in his loins spread through his blood. He got up and walked over to him, tossing his sphere up in the air and catching it.

"Bend over the table and spread your cheeks," he said.

After a slight hesitation, Attlad obeyed. Micah spat on

the sphere, warmed by his hands and shoved it, too, inside Attlad. "That will stretch you, make your virgin ass ready, when I decide to take you," he said. "Get me something to drink."

He watched Attlad straighten up and walk slowly and painfully over to the cupboard against one wall. He got out a bottle and come back again.

"Kneel on the floor and give me the bottle."

Attlad handed him the bottle and knelt, knees apart. His cock was harder now, Micah noticed. Micah tilted the bottle to his lips and took a long drink, then held it to Attlad's lips. He repeated this several times until his thirst was satisfied.

"Do you love this woman?" he asked.

Attlad looked up at him, astonished at the question. "This is a marriage. She will not be my P.B., not a love slave, or even a lover. Although I am the first male she has chosen. there will be others for her. I hear it is different where you come from."

"Yes, it's different. Will you …mate with her?"

"Why? When we want children, I will provide her with my sperm. That's enough. Is that different, too, where you come from?"

Micah nodded. "So this is like a business arrangement, then?"

"Of course. A very important business arrangement. Our backgrounds must be similar and we must be more or less of the same rank. We must preserve the line."

"You want a child," Micah murmured.

"Do you not want a son?"

"I hadn't ever considered it seriously," Micah said. He thought of Royal and grimaced. Royal had once talked about adopting a child.

"What has this to do with you and me?" Attlad said, puzzled.

Looking at him, it occurred to Micah that they had never really talked before. It was no wonder he was still in the dark about Kudite traditions! He felt again that unreasoning anger welling up. Weeks of frustration, humiliations and misunderstandings spilled over into action. He hit Attlad across the face with his open hand.

Attlad sprang at him with a snarl. The suddenness of the attack caught Micah by surprise and he was knocked to the floor before he recovered his wits. He quickly discovered he was at disadvantage, having his clothes on, whereas Attlad's naked body was hard to get a grip on. He was soon pinned to the floor. But he hadn't had all those hours of training with Grir for nothing. With a great effort, he gathered his strength, heaved Attlad backwards and pinned him between his legs. He felt Attlad's teeth sink into his calf, and only the leather of the trousers protected him. With a final squeeze of his muscular thighs he forced the air out of his opponent's chest and felt him gasp, his grip weakening. Micah grabbed the opportunity to fling him against the ground one more time, before releasing his grip just long enough to jump astride his naked chest. He raised his arm, hand ready to chop against his enemy's windpipe —

And paused.

This was not the enemy who lay beneath him, catching his breath. The red stain from his slap flared across the dark face. With a small sound of surrender, Micah leaned down and laid his mouth against the red mark, his tongue sliding over the rough stubble of the man's cheek, pushing between the man's lips, tasting his saliva. Attlad's tongue darted into his mouth, exploring, tasting, sliding down his throat. He felt Attlad's hands working at the buttons on his pants, working them open. Attlad's breath was hot against his face.

Micah rolled off the man and struggled out of his clothes. Within minutes he, too, was naked on the floor, clasped in sweating battle with Attlad as they kissed, and panted and struggled to release weeks of frustration, suffering and misunderstanding in each other's arms.

And then it didn't matter any more. It was suddenly clear how it would happen. Micah pulled away from the Kudite, one hand going to his engorged cock, this part of him that had been just recently returned to him.

"Squat in front of me," he signed with his other hand.

Attlad lay still for a moment, watching him, taking in the picture of the former slave, about to pleasure himself. With a grunt, he got into position, squatting in front of Micah with his feet apart, his balls swinging free. His great cock stood out before him, powerful, demanding. Watching it, Micah's eyes misted over with longing, but he forced himself to wait.

"Release the spheres from your ass," Micah signed. His eyes locked onto Attlad's as with a grunt, the Kudite expelled the metal globes from his anus. First one, then the other hit the floor with a dull thud and rolled along the wooden tiles. "Get up and lean over the table."

There was a long pause as the two men stared into each other's eyes. Micah felt a hot jangle of excitement pulse through him. His cock jerked in his hand. For a long moment, he thought he was going to lose the silent battle of wills. And then, he saw the hunger in the other man's eyes. Attlad looked away.

Slowly, with great dignity, the Kudite rose from his squat in one long, smooth movement. He walked to the table and leaned over, reaching for the far corners of the great expanse of black wood. Micah smiled in triumph as he kicked the legs wider apart. The marks of his belt glowed red and hot over the man's back and ass and thighs, and seeing them, Micah could no longer hold back. He saw the sweet eye of Attlad's ass, moist and vulnerable, open to him. He pushed the tip of his cock inside, heard the intake of breath, felt the ring of muscle tight around his flesh. He paused. Attlad was not used to being fucked and he needed time to relax. In a moment, Micah pushed further inside the velvet heat of the man, slowly, inexorably, until his balls, prickly now that the hair was growing back, finally hit the man's ass. Attlad was pulling in short sharp breaths of air, fighting against the pain. Micah waited for him to work through this phase. When he felt the man's hips shift, push back against him almost as if of their own accord, he withdrew a little, only to plunge in to the hilt once again. Slowly he began to pump in and out, his rhythm matched by the rocking motion of the man he was fucking. Faster and faster he rammed into him until his nuts churned. Hot molten cream whipped to a frenzy of need, exploded into the Kudites's quivering ass and Micah collapsed for a moment across Attlad's heaving back.

After a moment, Micah slid down the man's sturdy legs to the floor. His eyes blurred with tears as he looked at the big balls with their velvet covering of dark hair, drawn up close to the Kudite's body, full and hot, ready to burst with come. His moment of triumph had shown him plainly what he really wanted, what he had wanted all along; to kneel at his master's feet and suck his beautiful cock. And it was too late!

Attlad straightened up and turned around, his cock curving up to his belly it was so hard. He looked down at the kneeling man at his feet and put one hand on the blond fuzz covering his head. His other hand went to his cock, caressing the length of that beautiful hard shaft lovingly.

Micah felt the heat of his lust stain his face telltale red as he watched, mesmerized, as a string of pre-come drooled from the piss slit.

Attlad laughed, throwing his head back as his loud

mirth rolled around the large apartments, bouncing off the walls. Micah's blush deepened. He knew he could get to his feet now and walk away, and neither Attlad nor anyone else could stop him. He remained on his knees. Attlad's laughter died away. He was standing tantalizingly close, so close Micah could smell that sweet musk of mingled sweat and salt and urine that was uniquely his. Without being able to stop himself, he leaned forward, closer, closer, his mouth opening. He heard a wordless sound of longing escape from his throat and closed his eyes. Reverting to his months of training, his hands remained at his sides, not touching his own cock, which now began to swell as his lips slipped over the engorged head of Attlad's penis. He began to suck, even as the hard shaft slid further into his eager mouth, his cheeks expanding as the Kudite's meat filled him. He could feel Attlad's big hands on either side of his head and then the man slammed into his face with a guttural cry. He fucked him fiercely, jamming the Terran's face repeatedly into his hairy groin. His great cock grew impossibly large in Micah's throat, threatening to cut off his air supply, and then, with a shout, he came. Great spurting jets of come flooded Micah's mouth, forcing their way down his throat as he struggled to swallow it all. But this was impossible, as Attlad continued to shoot into him and come drooled from around the seal of his mouth still stretched in an O around the jerking cock. Even as the stream ceased and the huge rod began to dwindle, Micah continued to suck. He was happy to drain the last precious drop of Attlad's essence, that masculine elixir he had been yearning for for so long.

Attlad withdrew and pulled him to his feet. Without a word, he led the way to the sleeping chamber and together the two men tumbled onto the bed. They spent the rest of the afternoon making tempestuous love, at times gentle and tender, at times rough, verging on violent. By the time evening came, they both had scares and marks on their bodies. At last, sated and exhausted, they slept.

When they awoke, it was morning. Food and drink had been laid out invitingly on a small table beside the bed, along with a sheaf of blue papers and message strings. Attlad sat up and read them all, his face a mask of concentration. Then he sighed and put them back on the table and handed Micah a beaker of fermented honey and oranges.

As they ate and drank, sitting side by side on the bed, Attlad began to talk.

He talked about his loneliness when he lived here at the Citadel, the rivalry he never understood between himself and his brother. He talked about how coveted the role of warrior was among the Kudites and how the numbers were controlled, so only the very best could go. He had passed all the tests with flying colours. Kerdas had failed. Although he had been a great success in the Council, that failure rankled and Attlad was once again the target for his anger. According to the reports Attlad had just read, the young man who attacked him, the one Micah had killed, had held a minor office at the Council. Kerdas, apparently, had offered him a much higher office if he attacked his brother. Although the young man didn't realize it, he was not expected to succeed in his task. It was ludicrous to think that an inexperienced untrained young civilian would stand a chance against an experienced warrior. If by some fluke, he was successful, he would simply disappear in jail, set upon by other inmates, perhaps, or killed while trying to escape. Either way Kerdas would win. Attlad would be dead, or condemned to death for murder. Except that Micah was a witness, and he persevered until he made a difference.

"And now you are a free man again, what will you do?" Attlad asked at last.

Micah took a deep breath. "I would like to stay with

you," he said, "but I don't know if that's possible, now."

"What do you mean? I told you about the situation with Dadani. It is you I…hold dear," he finished awkwardly. He looked away, a man of action not comfortable talking about his feelings, especially with a man who had been his slave.

"It isn't just that," Micah said. He got out of bed and stretched, then picked up the glowing green stone and slipped it around his neck again. Attlad watched, his eyes narrowed. Micah felt a subtle shift in the air between them. He got back into bed and settled himself comfortably against the pillows. "I am a trained soldier," he said.

"You have been valuable to me," Attlad replied, after a moment. "On more than one occasion."

Micah took the man's hand and laid it on his cock, which nestled against his thigh. At Attlad's touch, the red dragon stirred.

Attlad took a drink of the heady mead, his hand still on Micah's cock. "The decision must be yours," he said at last.

"I know that. I am a free man, remember?" He smiled and touched the green stone. "If I return to you, I do so as a warrior."

Attlad put down the goblet and licked his lips slowly. "If you return to me, you do so as a love slave" he said, not looking at Micah. "You return as my P.B., Personal Bodyslave, Chento."

"A love slave who will ride beside you as your warrior companion," Micah amended. "You yourself mentioned this possibility long ago."

"I do not recall," Attlad said. He touched the metal collar around his neck, as if suddenly reminded of its presence. "If I agree, what is your decision?"

"The same as before," Micah said simply. "I am yours. I always have been."

Attlad let out his breath in a long sigh. Micah realized

he would probably have to pay for this bargaining session later on, but he didn't care. He had accomplished his goal.

"So be it." Attlad got up and took a small tool from a box on the table. Holding it under the prison collar, he cut through the metal and flung the hated symbol away. "The green stone," he said, holding out his hand to Micah. After a long moment of hesitation, Micah handed it over. As it touched Attlad's skin, it disintegrated, leaving only a fine powder on his hand. The transformation was complete.

Attlad began to get dressed. Micah picked up his shirt and started to put it on.

Suddenly a hand ripped it away from him. "No, Chento. Have you forgotten so soon? A slave goes naked in the house of his master."

Micah flushed, embarrassed to have forgotten.

Then the Kudite master took the large metal sphere Dadani had given him, placed it on the floor and pointed to it. "Sit on that, Chento."

"Yes, sir." It was hard to squat over the ball, his thigh muscles trembling as he tried to poise his body over the big sphere just so, knowing he was expected not to use his hands. He failed over and over, each time having to suffer his master's laughter as the ball rolled away from under his ass. But at last, he got the angle exactly right. The great sphere inched slowly up inside his lubed hole, where it stayed, a hard constant reminder of the master it belonged to. The pain mingled with the pleasure of knowing the apology sphere from Attlad's bride was now crammed inside his slave.

"Kneel on the floor at the foot of the bed."

Micah hurried to obey. Attlad picked up the Terran's leather belt from the floor and attached it to the bed post. Casually he bound Micah's wrists together behind his back, and then fastened him to the post in such a way that he was forced to lean forward, his shoulders pulled back, showing off his chest. Attlad smiled at his bound slave, noting with approval that the sleeping dragon had reawakened.

"Keep your ass hot and open," Attlad said, "and keep my dragon hard. When I get back, I'll give you a workout that'll make us both forget all about my brother and his treachery." With a final tweak of Micah's right tit, he went out of the room.

Micah watched his master leave. For hours he hung by his bound hands to the post, his ass stuffed, his cock always half hard as he drifted in and out of euphoria. He had what he wanted. He was utterly helpless, vulnerable, dependant on another man, a man who loved him. He could not believe that when he had first come to the Citadel, all he had wanted to do was to kill this man. Now he knew he would do anything in his power to please Attlad. He also knew his master would make him pay dearly for daring to bargain with him, but he didn't care. Micah Starion, the Nebula Warrior, was Chento once again. P.B. 500 had come home to his master.

Breinigsville, PA USA
07 September 2009
223653BV00001B/22/A